DON'T COUNT YOUR DEMONS BEFORE THEY HATCH

SUPERNATURAL MIDLIFE BOUNTY HUNTER

SHROUDED NATION BOOK 9

BRENDA TRIM

TIA DIDMON

Copyright © August 2023 by Brenda Trim and Tia Didmon
Editor:
Cover Art by Fiona Jayde

* * *

This book is a work of fiction. The names, characters, places, and incidents are products of the writers' imagination or have been used fictitiously and are not to be construed as real. Any resemblance to persons, living or dead, actual events, locales or organizations is entirely coincidental.

WARNING: The unauthorized reproduction of this work is illegal. Criminal copyright infringement is investigated by the FBI and is punishable by up to 5 years in federal prison and a fine of $250,000.

All rights reserved. With the exception of quotes used in reviews, this book may not be reproduced or used in whole or in part by any means existing without written permission from the authors.

❦ Created with Vellum

CHAPTER 1

"An extra-large dark roast and a breakfast wrap, please," I said, as the smell of melting cheese and coffee made my stomach rumble and my nostrils flare. That first sip of java in the morning was like ambrosia on the tongue. My mouth watered on the short drive from my bachelor suite to Danny's Bistro.

Jason chuckled as he inputted the order into the cash register. "I keep thinking you will change your order one of these days, but you never do." He looked so much like his father Danny, that I had to remind myself we were in our forties and I wasn't a teen ordering from his father.

I used to order the Rinters' cookies and doughnuts back in the day with chocolate milk. Unlike the supernaturals in town, the mundanes had no idea about my heritage and had always been kind to me. It was no wonder I chose a mundane life and husband. Those choices were long gone, I reminded myself. The difference now was that I was starting to accept the supernatural world had its perks. Namely, a warlock with a sexy body and magic for days.

I winked at Jason. "Why mess with a good thing? But you can add a chocolate chip cookie for old times' sake."

Jason chuckled and added the cookie to my order. His white apron was thick in the middle, likely from the array of sweets his family was known for. "You have become one of my best customers, Faith. You're welcome to call in your order, and I will have it ready for you when you arrive."

The young girl with long brown hair in a ponytail and a similar apron glanced at the screen and began preparing my breakfast behind the counter. She put eggs, cheese, and sausage in the wrap before popping it in a toaster oven.

"And miss our morning chats? Those are almost as good as your coffee." Teasing him was as fun as the food was good.

"You always had that wit about you. If I wasn't happily married, I would chase you for sure."

The girl grunted. "Gross, Dad."

We both laughed, and I had to admit I loved the camaraderie of the Rinter family. I had met Jason's wife, Darla, a few times now. She was just as kind as her husband. I took the small brown bag with the cookie in it and the coffee before paying for my order. The wrap came out of the small oven and Jason's daughter wrapped it tightly after adding the homemade chipotle sauce I loved.

My phone chimed as I exited the bistro to the busy main street in town. The businesses on Raven Street were not open yet, but Danny's was always lined up at this time of day. The main street in Ravenholde liked to start its day the same way I did. Yeah, Jason's father, Danny, had created a bakery goldmine. His wife, Lorraine, still baked many of the sweets they sold. Danny still visited his son at the cafe often. Though he mostly chatted with customers and praised his granddaughter.

I took a sip of my coffee and let the hot liquid burn its way down to my throat while settling the caffeine withdrawal that I started my day with. Although it did nothing to soothe the butterflies in my stomach as I read the text from Greyson.

We need to talk.

Four simple words, but they could mean so much. I had postponed my search for the shadow creature who stole the shard from me to help find Mina. Rescuing Eve's daughter had taken priority, but I still had a missing fae, vampire, and shifter. I wanted the prick who had attacked us at Eve's store. That bastard was going to get a saber up the backside. I meant my newly-sharpened sword, not me.

Still, the sexy warlock who invaded my dreams and made my succubus purr was just as important to me as my hunt for a traitor. I hit his contact, and it rang once before he picked up.

"I didn't expect you to respond so fast."

I moved to the front of Danny's bistro, so I was out of the way of the pedestrians on the sidewalk. I leaned against the large glass window. "I was going to call you. Do you want me to pop over now, before I get caught up in my search?"

"I would appreciate that. Do you want breakfast?"

"I'm at Danny's Bistro. I got a wrap, but I can grab you something if you want."

"No. I already ate. See you in a bit." He hung up, and I put my phone away.

I threaded my way through the small tables that sat in front of the bistro and down the sidewalk to the black Corvette I was driving. I had gotten it from the doppels yesterday when I popped by to see my grandfather and Cal.

It unlocked automatically as I approached with the key fob in my pocket. Modern technology was amazing. Sitting down, I put the key in the ignition. The sports car didn't have the button start like the Mercedes, but it was such a fun drive. Despite the suggestive license plates, my grandfather's garage of infinite vehicles was becoming one of my favorite perks.

I pulled into traffic, which wasn't too heavy this early in the morning. It would get more congested, closer to nine, when the retail stores began to open. I hit a few red lights before turning onto Granger. The houses were all large and most were painted white, with perfectly manicured lawns. The properties closest to Raven Street were owned by the empowered but several businesses were still mundane owned or operated. It was only a few short blocks to Lokell, and I parked in Greyson's driveway soon after turning onto his street. My heart was racing, and my hormones started hopping.

His front door opened, and he exited the white house with black trim. The rosebushes were in full bloom, and I smiled at the man that made my heart flutter. His simple white T-shirt and black casual pants made him even sexier than when he dressed up. He glanced at my license plate before he took a sip from the blue mug he held in his hand.

I knew what he was laughing at. The license plate 2SEXY4U and was one of Carnell's tamer ones. I grabbed my wrap and coffee. "I know the plate is tacky, but it was this or FUCKME."

Greyson held his coffee away from his lips as he choked. "He put that on a license plate?"

I shrugged. "He is a succubus demon. It pays to advertise, I guess."

Greyson tapped his chest. "Then I think you made the right choice. That would be a little…"

"I know. I have issues with some of the choices he makes." I ascended the stairs to his home and went on my tiptoes to give him a kiss. "Hi."

He grabbed the doorknob to his home and opened it. "After you."

I entered the living room with the pristine white couches and lavender throw pillows. I would never have been able to keep furniture like this clean. Everything was perfectly arranged, including the picture of him and Victoria that sat on the mantel. My place back in Cincinnati had many pictures of me, Liam, and Luke. Since my son was still living in our house, I never took anything but my clothes. That reminded me there were still some items I wanted to retrieve when things settled down.

He led me through the living room to the kitchen and motioned for me to sit at the large oak table with an empty fruit bowl at its center. I grabbed a seat and began to unwrap my breakfast. "Thanks," I said before taking a bite. The cheese and sausage melted on my tongue, and I moaned a little as Greyson sat down opposite me.

He placed his blue mug on the table and crossed his legs. "I was hoping we could talk about us."

Yeah, this conversation was long overdue. His words made me so nervous I swallowed my food even though it hadn't been chewed enough and caught in my throat. I coughed, trying to clear it. "I agree."

Greyson leaned forward. "I like you, Faith. A lot. I know neither of us was looking for this, but here we are. While I may have thought our attraction was pheromone based at first, it's safe to say that I am attracted to you regardless of any external forces."

My wrap crinkled as I put it down. "I like you, too. You're sexy, funny… and that isn't the succubus. Honestly, I can't even think of being with anyone else."

Greyson put his hand over mine. "I know. That's what scares me."

My heart fluttered. "You don't want me to be faithful? Or for us to be exclusive? I have only been with two men in my life. I don't know anything else."

"I have no desire for anyone else, and I don't want you with another guy. But if you are injured and I am not available. What will you do? Dying isn't an option and with you traveling to other cities to track down these bounties… I fear for you."

I wasn't sure what he was trying to say. Was this a let's keep it casual talk or I think it would be better if we split up speech? I wasn't used to either. My husband had pursued me like a relentless pit bull and had never let go. I had never doubted where I stood with Luke and that had hit harder when I killed him.

I pulled my hand away slowly. "You don't want to see me anymore?"

Greyson swore under his breath and grabbed my hand, pulling it toward him. "I am terrible at this. It's been too many years since I have had to define a relationship. You know I want us to be exclusive. I already told you that, but I want more. I was hoping we could tell our sons we are seeing someone. Mattias is away at college right now, but when he returns, I was hoping to introduce you."

Man, had I pegged that convo wrong. I was sure I looked like a deer caught in headlights. I cleared my throat and wrapped my hand around my coffee. Getting a weapon out right now would be bad form. "Why did you say that stuff about me being hurt and about being able to get to you? You're a warlock, and my grandfather has access to a portal. I would never betray you."

Greyson sighed. "If you are hurt. You call me first. I am creating a bracelet for you. A panic button, if you will. Just for emergencies. Think of it as a last resort method. I am well aware of your skills and that you can take care of yourself, but I need some peace of mind."

People often assumed a bounty hunter like me was not a girly girl. And in most cases, they were right. I preferred weapons to fancy clothes and expensive jewelry, but the idea of him making me something really appealed to me. "I would be happy to wear anything you make."

"Good. I want people to know we are together. Hopefully, that will stop Rhain and Kormack from hitting on you."

I arched an eyebrow. "Kormack has hit on me once. How many times has he hit on you over the years?"

Greyson released my hand. "Perhaps that was a bad example. But Kormack was always respectful of my marriage, and his flirting was... more teasing in nature."

I chuckled. "You have to give the empusa props for having good taste in men."

He took a sip of his coffee. "Perhaps, but he never considered a single female until you."

I grabbed my wrap. "It must be my winning personality," I said before taking a bite.

Greyson smirked. "I am sure that's it." He frowned. "Listen, I have been working on a shield for you. It's always more difficult with a non-magic user, but I want to make the panic bracelet first if that's okay with you."

"Sure. I need to prioritize finding Dagna and see if she is the one who created that shadow thing. It could hide anybody, and that is plain scary."

Greyson thrummed his fingers on the table. "I agree. She needs to be questioned, but don't assume she has anything to do with the loss of the shard. Eve assumed Dagna was working for Rerek and she wasn't. That witch has her own agenda and may have nothing to do with the theft of the tokens or the missing supernaturals."

"She was hired to make nullifying coins and Odin is pissed she is cutting in on his dark magic game. He definitely skirts the line, but he would never be complicit in murder or abduction. She needs to be taken off the streets."

"I agree. But the Fade sisters are more powerful than you realize. Their mother's story is sealed by the council, but she feared that one day her daughters would put their petty differences aside and unite."

"You know the Fade sisters' history?" I asked.

"Yes. I already asked Carnell if I could relay the information. He gave me council approval."

I put my wrap down and grabbed my coffee. "Let's hear it."

Greyson leaned back in his seat. "First, you have to understand that Kora Fade was a powerful witch. There is little known about her lover. It was unusual for a witch not to marry the

CHAPTER 2

Greyson sighed. "That's a long story, and I'm not sure anyone knows the truth of it. However, I can't say I agree with trying to bind a witch based on a vision. Rumors are Kora saw something and felt she had to stop it from happening. Maybe Kora was unstable and her actions caused a ripple effect. It's a case of the chicken and the egg. We only have Glinda's diary to go by and that is written with her perception of the truth."

That wasn't exactly reliable. Glinda was a psycho. "What kind of ritual binds a witch's powers? I wasn't aware you could do that?"

"It's very difficult and unethical to bind a fully-developed witch or warlock, but Kora was attempting to do it to her adolescent daughters. Glinda was only fourteen when Kora tried for the first time. She should not have had the power to block her mother, but after several attempts and many years, Kora had to accept that no matter what she did, her daughters' powers could not be removed."

My stomach dropped out hearing his words. "This ritual is bad, I take it?"

"Dark magic of this magnitude requires a death. While it's possible she was using animal hearts, we suspect the string of mundane murders over the span of a decade to belong to Kora. Still, there is no proof, so I wouldn't go around saying that to anyone."

A shudder of revulsion worked its way through me. "Okay. I was about to ask why the council wouldn't attempt to bind Glinda's powers, but the human sacrifice answers that question."

"We shy away from such magic. I doubt it would work on Glinda if we didn't. Even if the entire council brought their powers to bear, they couldn't do much. Especially now. She and her sister are far more powerful now than they were when they averted their mother's spells."

I glanced at the copper canisters beside the coffeemaker. Greyson seemed to avoid answering me, and that wasn't like him. He was the first to ask the tough questions when it came to our relationship, so why the evasiveness now? "You don't have to answer me if you don't want to. I know this magic stuff isn't my purview. If you prefer to tell Eve and have her relay."

Greyson shook his head. "No. It isn't that. Kora had Dagna… cut symbols into Glinda's chest and back. She maimed her oldest daughter. Since the shifter alpha she enamored had no knowledge of her wounds, we believe she glamored them when she was with him."

I swallowed hard. "Dagna sliced up her own sister?"

"Kora was unbalanced. She beat Dagna within an inch of her life and told her it would happen every time she disobeyed. As a result, the sisters were not close, to say the least. We weren't surprised when Dagna left town, prior to her sister's incarceration."

"That's horrible. I have no love for Glinda, but Kora likely created the monster and left us dealing with her."

"That is what the previous council believed as well. It's the reason she was not sentenced to death. Her mother abused her so badly that it's hard to hold her responsible for her actions. In the end, she was found criminally insane."

"Yeah, I can see that. Clearly, Dagna didn't escape that madness. I bet she is just as imbalanced as her sister."

"You're right about that. However, she was never involved in Glinda's ploy for power. We found no mention of Dagna in the journal and the few references from when they were younger held contempt. The council believed Glinda would kill her sister if given the choice."

Talk about a dysfunctional family. This one sounded like the definition of one. "Maybe that's her end game. I think Dagna is working on her own agenda. Maybe she wants her sister dead. There could be a lot more to the Fade family story."

"That's more than possible. Glinda was tight-lipped about her true agenda when she was apprehended and Dagna had disappeared."

I huffed. "Wow. Psycho mom passes on all the good genes. Too bad they weren't more like the father. He had to be better than Kora."

"We don't know much about him. He died shortly after Dagna was born."

"How?" I was naturally suspicious of everyone, but that information set off every one of my alarm bells.

"He died in a car accident. Rare for a warlock, but it can happen. Especially if he was being siphoned." That made me think of what Caton had done to Eve and set my teeth on edge.

I folded my arms. "Or maybe he had a nullifying coin on him. The kind that makes your magic go on the fritz."

Greyson's eyes widened. "Holy shit. That's possible. Let me pull up the report on his death. I will get back to you on that."

I took the last bite of my breakfast wrap, but it was cold. The Fade sisters' story was cruel, but it had garnered my attention, and my food and drink had paid the price. When I grabbed my coffee cup and put it back on the table with a look of disgust, Greyson waved his hand over my cup.

Steam erupted from the opening of the lid, and I smiled. "I knew you weren't just a pretty face. I hope you put official mug warmer on your resume."

"Unlikely." His eyes held the laughter he tried to hide in his voice.

I grabbed my cell phone when it beeped and looked at the text. "Shit. I have to go."

Greyson stood up. "What is it?"

"A witch was abducted. I have to meet Carnell at Club Bliss."

Greyson's gray eyes flickered. "Do you know who?"

"No. But I will let you know once I have more details." I grabbed my coffee and dashed to the door. I was outside bolting for the Corvette before I realized I should have kissed Greyson goodbye. He would understand my urgency and wouldn't hold it against me. There was a certain security in knowing how someone felt about you. I appreciated he was more forthcoming with his feelings than I was. It gave me the gift of that security.

I got into the driver's seat and started the engine. My tires screeched on the pavement as I pulled out of Greyson's driveway. I wouldn't be surprised if he got a complaint about the rubber I peeled. I was racing toward Raven Street and my grandfather's club less than a minute after receiving his text.

The traffic was fairly dense after I turned onto Raven Street, and I got several dirty looks for weaving through traffic like a madwoman. They could stuff it. I had no idea who had been abducted and my call to Eve had gone straight to voice mail. Nishi wasn't picking up either. My heart was racing. I could understand Nishi wanting some alone time to heal after Nathan's death. That didn't explain Eve. As wrong as I knew it was, I prayed Lucinda or anyone but Eve was the witch that had been taken.

I pulled into the alley that led behind Club Bliss and glanced

My heart slowed to a normal rate as my worry for Eve diminished. "Where is this store?"

"The Magnetic Boutique is down the street. They said they chose it for its location, but we all know it's because Nancy is one of Lucinda's sophisticates. The poor girl doesn't jump without asking Lucinda how high. She dresses like her, and sounds like her."

"Charming. Do you know where she was abducted from?" I silently thanked the gods for answering my prayer. I would look for the witch, but I needed Eve. Her advice and potions had become part of my bounty-hunting repertoire. Not to mention she was one of my closest friends.

"Lucinda wants to meet with you to organize a search and…"

My leather creaked as I stood up. "I will work for you. I will even help with council business and find a witch regardless of who her friends are, but let me be clear. Under no circumstances will I tolerate that tramp. Silicone Barbie can stay the fuck away from me if she wants me to help find Nancy. That bitch is awful to Eve and Caton can burn in hell. My saber almost slipped from its scabbard and through her neck when we were looking for Mina. Had Eve's daughter not been present, I am not sure I would have contained myself."

One corner of Carnell's mouth lifted. "Well. I am glad you were able to restrain yourself."

I wasn't one to dwell on my more predatory responses. "I was drawing it when Hunter noticed. He gave me the alpha stare, and I backed down. Nobody else noticed. Just so I'm clear. Lucinda is not safe around me."

Carnell stared at me for some time. I wasn't sure if he was disappointed or concerned. "I understand your protective streak, Faith. It is an admirable quality. I need you to remember that while Lucinda is difficult, she has never broken the law."

I placed both hands on his desk and leaned forward. "She cut Eve from the coven, assuming it would kill her. That. Is. Murder."

I emphasized the last three words so my grandfather was clear about my position on that.

Carnell frowned. "While I agree with you, Lucinda is the elected leader of the witches. She had the right to expel Eve, but that decision has backfired tenfold. Eve is using you, Nishi, and Hunter to ground her. And because none of you have magic that makes you draw from her, she is far more powerful."

"I, for one, am glad Eve found a way to use us. I hope Lucinda falls on her plastic backside. She is the worst person to be leading the coven. Eve would never go back to them, but there has to be a better candidate than Lucinda."

"I don't believe a witch can be returned to a coven after being severed, but we have no control over other factions of the supernatural world. If the law is not broken, we must abide by the council's rules."

I waved my hand dismissively. "Whatever. Just don't put me in the same room with her unless you want her to get a beat down."

Carnell looked exasperated with me. "I have asked Greyson to meet you at the Magnetic Boutique. We need to know if the portal is safe. I have confirmed it is operational and we need to know if she allowed someone to use it."

I stood up and straightened my leather jacket. "I just left his house. Him, I have no problem meeting to check if Nancy was abducted from the boutique."

Carnell leaned back, which made his white shirt gape open. I hadn't noticed it was unbuttoned to the navel until he moved. "Have you discussed a more permanent relationship status?" He held up his hand. "Before you ask, Greyson came to speak with me. He wanted to ensure he would be… enough for you. In the demonic sense."

My shoulders sagged. "Did you put that nonsense in his head about me needing sex to regenerate? That I would die if he wasn't available."

Carnell frowned. "No. You will always be part human and

even though your demon side is active, you do not have the same appetites as your pure-blood brethren. I assured him you would never betray his trust. It is not in your nature. Neither human nor demon."

Just when I thought I couldn't feel like more of an idiot. "Oh." Yep, always a smooth talker when I was eating crow. "Thanks."

"I can ensure you have access to your warlock if needed. Eve's suppressant has worked well for you. I do not know why he is concerned with this aspect of your nature. You are succubi, so the sex must be fabulous."

"Oh, my, god. Stop. I am not having a sex talk with my grandfather." Bile churned in my stomach as I fought the urge to run away screaming *na na na na, I can't hear you*.

Carnell gave me a knowing look. "We have always given instruction to the next generation. I can have another give you some tips if…"

"The sex is amazing. Dammit, you are relentless." It was easier to give him some of what he wanted.

"I only have your best interests at heart." His tone was low and there was no deception. Was it possible my grandfather loved me that much?

"Sorry. I know you do. This is all just… a lot sometimes. Being part demon when I think like a human."

Carnell looked away. "I have often wondered what monogamy would be like. I wish I could try it."

I had thought a witch abduction was the biggest surprise of my day. How wrong could a demon be? "You would entertain a monogamous relationship?"

CHAPTER 3

Carnell was quiet for a moment and sat down. The concept of monogamy and my incubus grandfather went together like oil and water. "I asked Eve to see if she could create a suppressant that would work for me. I am an elder of our race, so it's more difficult to create the potency needed. But even if it worked for a few weeks. Think about how intimate you could become with one person. To enjoy their company and not... need to end up in bed. I have often envied the elderly mundanes. When their relationship seems to be about togetherness and shared interest without the drive to procreate."

My shoulders sagged as I saw a side of my grandfather I didn't believe existed. This Carnell was vulnerable and sad, wistful, and somewhat alone. I had assumed he loved his carefree life. The thought that he had no choice in the matter hurt. It never occurred to me that his life depended on him embracing. Young succubus and incubus probably loved their lifestyle. Not unlike a teenager or new adult who wasn't ready for a committed relationship. But what happened when they matured? Did they all envy the mortal life of a mundane? The evolution of life and relationships that made ours so special because they were finite. "I never considered what it would be like to be a full-blood. To be forced to have multiple partners."

Carnell smiled sadly. "Most of our species relish our lifestyle and don't think as I do. Perhaps it is the years I have spent in the human realm that have changed me. Maybe it's just old age."

I grunted. "You may be old, but you don't look it. Even Mrs. Harriet thinks you are hot."

Carnell arched an eyebrow. "She is a lovely woman. Her mint chocolate chip cookies are to die for."

I leaned forward. "Don't even think about it. While I am sure you would give her the time of her life, you could give her a heart attack."

Carnell chuckled. "I would never risk the loss of her cookies." I chose not to comment that he was more than willing to entertain my landlady if her baked goods weren't in jeopardy.

He glanced down when his phone chimed. "Greyson will meet you at the Magnetic Boutique in fifteen minutes. He just arrived at Scorchwood prison. The barrier is hell on reception. He's returning now."

"I'm surprised he got your message at all."

"While his security is second to none. He is the source. He has access to this entire town. In some ways, he is more powerful than any of us."

I stood up, but paused. "Your comments about monogamy surprised me."

Carnell was looking down, and I couldn't see his eyes. He ran his finger over a white manila folder with no writing on it. "You would be surprised what you don't know about me or our family."

It was impossible not to detect the sadness in his voice. "Then it's time I found out."

Carnell's sea-green eyes snapped to mine. There was doubt and hopefulness I hadn't seen since I was a child. Had I caused that? Had my inability to get over my childhood jaded me so much I hurt those who loved me?

"Your priority is finding Nancy and seeing if the portal has been compromised, but I hope you begin to see that the supernatural world can hold just as much beauty as the mundane one."

I nodded before exiting his library and heading for the elevator. It was open, and I was sure Dran had sent it back up. The doppels were so considerate and kind. They had become the big brothers I had yearned for as a child. The doors closed as soon as I hit the button for the main floor.

Dran was waiting for me when the door chimed open and winked before leading me down the hallway to the alley exit. I glanced at the door that led to the basement where the doorway to the Underworld was located. I couldn't help but wonder how the new Sharun was doing.

I continued on when Dran opened the glass door. I would have to check on Sharun sometime soon. I followed as Dran led me to my Corvette before opening the door. I waved goodbye to him before glancing up at the gargoyle on the roof and starting the engine.

The drive to the boutique was fast, and I regretted not walking when I realized I had to circle back to park. After waiting for a blue station wagon to exit a stall on Raven Street, I got out of the car and approached the Magnetic Boutique.

The sign was flipped to closed, which was unusual when everything else on Raven was a bustle of activity. The storefront consisted of two large picture windows that allowed a passerby to see the perfectly organized high-end merchandise inside. The white Victorian-styled door sat between the pink walls below the windows. The pastel color was in contrast to the muted colors of the adjacent stores.

I approached the door and tried the brass knob. It was locked, so I cupped my hands together and peeked through the glass. The store was long, and I couldn't get a good look at the back where the portal was reportedly built.

"Need some help?" Greyson asked as he leaned toward me.

I smacked him playfully in the stomach. "Never sneak up on me like that. I am armed."

Greyson chuckled, then reached around me to put his hand on the doorknob. He turned it, and it made a clicking noise before he opened the door. He pushed it wide and released the handle. "After you."

"You're like a master key or something, aren't you?"

"Something like that. Even I can't ward myself. Magic doesn't work that way."

I entered the store and glanced at the perfectly arranged racks on either side of the aisle. They were all organized by style and size. The shelves above them had a nice display of purses, matching wallets, and various high-end shoes. The tables in the middle had an array of folded T-shirts and scarves. I tried not to react when I noticed a plain white T-shirt was over two-hundred dollars.

"I can get the same thing at the thrift store for under five bucks," I observed before I could censor myself.

Greyson tried to hide his smile as he walked toward the cash register and changing rooms at the back. There was a door behind the sales counter which I assumed was a storage room. He opened the door to change room three, making the place fill with mist. "The portal is operational, but it has not been activated. I am installing a second security measure. Only a portal crystal holder will be able to unlock the door. Nancy should have had me set this up before the portal was operational. We're lucky there wasn't an incident." He took out his phone and sent off a text. "I have asked Eve to pop over. I want her permission to make a change to the portal protections for the council."

While Caton and Lucinda were up in arms about Eve's

involvement in the council accessibility, Greyson was happy to work with his friend. He appreciated Eve's skill and expertise, and I wished the others could see what a rare gift she was.

I moved behind the counter to see if there was any sign of a struggle. The counter was a pink color that matched the walls and was neatly organized with white pen holders and white bags with the store logo printed on them. Finding nothing out of the ordinary, I went through the door behind the counter.

The storage room was simple and was painted a plain white. The first shelf was full of various shoes and sizes Nancy had available. But the next was full of extra bags, gift boxes and tissue. She had some Christmas decorations and various cleaning supplies, but like the front, there was nothing to indicate she was taken from the boutique. I jogged back to the cash register and hit a button on the thing. It beeped on and I noticed the digital time and date.

While I had no idea how to work her cash register, I was sure she had to close out the sales and start them new for the next business day. I opened the drawer beneath the counter and found a black ledger. After opening it to the last entry, I found Nancy had closed the day before and there was nothing filled out for this morning.

I rummaged through the drawer but found nothing to help with my investigation and looked up when the front door opened. Eve smiled as she closed the front door. "You looking for a new outfit?" I asked.

Eve ran her hand over her thin black jacket. "I can't afford this place. Besides, it's a little too…"

"Lucinda? Yeah, I know."

Greyson turned as Eve approached the back of the store. Her long brown hair cascaded over one shoulder, making her look more like a model than the young girls in the photos on the wall. "Thanks for coming. I want your magic as part of the security since the portal takes the user to shifter lands. I was also hoping for your approval for Faith. Carnell has authorized a crystal for her, and I plan to give her my access to the council chambers with your authority."

Eve nodded. "Absolutely. Hunter said she can enter shifter lands at her leisure, which honestly surprised me. He has given the same to Nishi."

I had a pretty good idea why Hunter would authorize me and Nishi on shifter land. He wanted his girl close by and wouldn't want her to feel isolated from her friends. It would mean more time for her on pack lands.

Eve glanced at the third changing room. By then the mist had dissipated and it looked identical to the other two. "This is the portal? I was expecting it to be in the storage room in the back. Why is it out front? Nancy sells to mundane clientele."

Greyson nodded. "I wasn't excited about that myself, but the portal will only activate with a crystal and unless I am working on the system, it only activates when the door is closed. There is no sound, so a mundane could be in the next stall and not see or hear anything. I've done what I can to keep it as safe as possible. However, it isn't ideal."

Eve crossed her arms over her chest. "I think Nancy should close to the mundane public an hour early and make sure the supernaturals come after then to travel. I have no idea what Lucinda was thinking."

I grunted. "She was thinking that she's a queen and can do what she wants. It's not good that she has complete control over Nancy. In the end, it gives her complete control over the council chamber portal. And makes her feel important. She needs that more than ever with Caton making goo-goo eyes at you."

Greyson's eyebrow shot up as his gray eyes flickered. "Caton has finally realized what a colossal mistake he made?"

Eve pulled at the collar of her cotton shirt. "I'm sure it was just the stress of Mina's abduction. He will go back to his self-centered, jackass status soon."

Greyson huffed. "Don't be so sure. It was only a matter of time until he saw what the rest of us did. He gave up fillet mignon for chuck roast and he is beginning to choke on it."

I chuckled as Eve's cheeks tinged with red. "I'm sure it's just a phase," she said.

"I agree with Greyson on that one," I said before leaning on the counter. "I don't think Nancy was taken from here. I need to get more information about her day-to-day activities. Lucinda wasn't sure when she was taken. Nancy closed her shop last night and cashed out, so we are looking at a grab-and-go between 6 pm and early this morning. I may have to check her residence next."

Greyson pulled a crystal from his pocket. It was white as it was currently inert. It would glow purple when the portal activated. The council members had permanent crystals, so theirs were green when activated. "This is for you, Faith. Carnell has authorized you to have access to his home portal. You have the same... well, technically more access than the other council members."

"Is that a green crystal?"

"Yes."

"Why would I have a green crystal?"

Eve winked. "Because the demons, shifters, and hunters trust you. Rhain said you were welcome to visit him anytime as well."

I made a gagging sound before Eve laughed. "I'd rather bathe in bacon grease. I'd feel less oily, afterward."

Greyson's eyes sparkled. "Smooth talker."

I winked at him. "It's part of my charm. Does Lucinda know I have an all-access pass to the chambers?"

Eve's lip twitched. "I am surprised you didn't hear the screeching from here. She would have confronted you, but she wants Nancy found and knows you are her best chance. After she is recovered, you can expect a confrontation."

My vision wavered and both Eve and Greyson stepped toward me as my hand went to my saber. "I look forward to it."

Greyson and Eve shared a glance before she said, "Faith, your eyes flickered."

"I'm pissed. Lucinda better come armed if she wants to go a round with me."

Greyson touched my shoulder. "It wasn't just that. It was... I don't know. Your other side poking through."

My muscles tensed. "Which one?"

Eve clutched her black purse closer to her. "Hunter's eyes do that when he's angry or... aroused, but you have never displayed any shifter traits before."

I recalled the conversation with Orek. He had been the first to mention my shifter side. Apparently, he wasn't going to be the last. "I can't explain it. All I know is that witch brings out the worst in me."

Eve sighed. "She brings out the worst in everyone. Just don't do anything that will get you in trouble with the council."

"I can't make any promises. If she crosses a single line with me, she will reap the consequences."

Eve stepped closer to me. "I know she is a back-stabbing bitch, but I don't want you to get in trouble because she is jealous of my power."

My friend was wonderful and naïve. She truly didn't see it was a lot more than her power, Lucinda was jealous of. "I have to check out Nancy's residence. Do you have the address?"

Greyson sent me a text. "I just sent it to you. There were no disturbances in the area, and she lives close to Caton and Lucinda, so she is under their protection."

I grabbed my phone when it rang, after checking the caller ID. "Hey, Carnell."

"I need you to go to the council chambers. I think I found the scroll that depicts the ritual you keep encountering. I may be able to give you a location for the next one."

My heart fluttered at the thought of catching my next bounty in the act. "I'm on my way." I hung up the phone and went to Greyson before giving him a quick kiss.

His eyes searched mine. "Where are you off to?"

I smiled. "Hopefully, a stakeout."

CHAPTER 4

The drive to the Freecrest pack lands was quiet once I got out of the downtown core of Ravenholde. My Corvette jumped when I pressed the gas pedal. The road that led to the entrance of Hunter's territory was beautiful, with dense forest lining both sides of the road. There wasn't a street sign or speed limit. There was also nothing to indicate when I passed into pack territory. There wasn't a defining line between city-owned land. When two attractive men exited the forest and one held his hand up, I knew I was on their property. I recognized Reed from the council chambers, but not his partner.

I slowed down and rolled down my window as he approached. "Hey. Fancy meeting you here," I said to Reed and his dark-haired companion.

Reed looked a little older than his companion, but both had dark brown eyes and hair. They were muscular and fit. And based on their lack of shoes and a shirt they had been running in their wolf form. Hunter once told me the shifters had stashes of clothing close to the road. It wasn't for their benefit, either. They were unconcerned about nudity within the pack. The mundanes thought the land was privately owned and had no knowledge of the supernatural. Shifters didn't possess magic, so they had to gear up if they ran into a mundane or non-shifter.

"Hi, Faith. Carnell told us you were coming. Despite that, Hunter let us know he has given you access to the chambers at your convenience. We have beefed up security now that the chambers are on our land and will be stopping all vehicles that cross into our territory. I'm just giving Ian a rundown on the new protocols."

I nodded with a smile. "I have never been there before. Eve explained where it is, but do I need to stop somewhere and check in?"

"Hunter gave you access as well which means you can take the main road. It leads to the new council chambers, as well as his residence," Reed said.

Ian grunted. "He gave an all-access pass to a cat? That's pathetic."

Reed turned fast and grabbed Ian by the throat. He had the startled young man pinned to the roof of my car before I could blink. I assumed my speed had come from my demon side, but the shifters were far more agile than I gave them credit for.

"Don't you ever disrespect Faith again. She is looking for your friend Kyle. More importantly, she is under Hunter's protection. If anyone touches her, they win a sparring round with the alpha. Considering his wolf is double the size of yours and your skills are a toddler's in comparison, I recommend you avoid the experience. Not to mention Hunter has been a little testy lately with all the turmoil surrounding Eve, the council, and the pack. He may accidentally kill you." Reed's rage bled through his words.

Ian placed his hand over Reed's wrist. "I'm sorry. It won't happen again."

Eve had told me about her first trip to shifter lands to help an elderly woman infected with the virus. The men who had attacked her and almost killed her were in wolf form, so she didn't know all their names. This young prick was likely one of them. Hunter thought he needed to protect me, which was sweet, really. And I would never touch one of his people out of respect for him and Eve, but Ian was rash. I wouldn't approach him while I was in their territory; however, he would venture into mine, eventually. And Saber had an eidetic memory. Thinking of my bounty hunter persona as a different person entirely made it a lot easier to deal with jerks like Ian. I could unleash Saber on them without guilt. It was my job.

Reed released Ian and moved to the side of the road. I winked at Ian. "Come by Club Bliss sometime. I will buy you a drink." And teach you what I can do with an assortment of weapons. Yeah, I didn't voice the last part, but I was pretty sure Reed got the meaning. He sighed as Ian smirked.

I followed the road to the council chambers and could see some side roads that led to an array of houses. I knew there were numerous shifters on the massive property, but I would visit none of them except Hunter's. It was ironic that my shifter heritage kept popping up when I couldn't feel anything from my so-called cat.

The sign marked council chambers was beside a parking area in front of it. I could see the building looked identical to the original. Eve had told me that while I couldn't see it, there was a barrier around the magical chambers.

Greyson had already programmed my biometrics into the shield so I wouldn't feel it when I passed through, but she assured me that most of the council members could not see the area that surrounded the new building.

Nishi was still mourning Nathan's loss and Eve was helping Greyson at the boutique, so I was glad my grandfather would be there to intervene if Caton and Lucinda were on site. Man. I prayed they had better things to do than take an interest in my investigation.

There was a walkway between the fence that surrounded the building. It was a new addition to the chambers, and looked more like the rustic architecture of the shifter homes than the Roman building with an ornate facade with intricate carvings on the facia above the Roman columns. There were over a dozen supporting the front of the building, and I wished the council had taken the area into account. The style was woefully out of place in the natural area.

I jogged up the steps and opened the large door that led to the chambers. While the outside looked to be complete, the inside was still under construction. Several shelving units sat in the middle of a large four-story room as if there was a dispute on where to put them. I weaved my way through the rows of columns to the long wooden table on the dais with a live edge of greenery growing from it. I wasn't sure if they had been able to save the last one or recreated it, but the magic board was lit up behind the table and I knew the portal was operational, though it was currently inactive.

Lucinda sat beside Caton at the table and was arguing with him about something. She hadn't noticed me until I approached the table. Her eyes bulged when her gaze landed on me. "Who summoned you? And how did you get in here?" Her eyes assessed me, making it hard to control my fists. "Greyson had no right to give you full access to the chambers. It's a gross breach of security." Her comment made me wonder if she had a charm that allowed her to read minds. I would have to ask Eve about that possibility.

"I couldn't give a rat's ass about coming here. You want to find Nancy yourself? Be my guest." I turned to walk from the building as Caton stood.

"Wait, Faith," Caton said. The jackass was being reasonable? The world really had turned topsy-turvy.

I stopped and turned to him, with a sneer of contempt as an oval white light, tinged with blue on the rim, formed beside the table. Carnell stepped through as if he had just left a photo shoot.

He smiled when he saw me, but it didn't take long for him to understand the dynamic in the room. "What is going on?"

Lucinda pointed at me. "The bounty hunter should fetch the missing members of our community, but she should only have a temporary crystal. Her having full access to the chambers is ridiculous. She walked right in here. She didn't even portal."

Carnell sighed. The exasperation on his face made him appear older. "She was investigating Nancy's abduction. Greyson and Eve are increasing security at the boutique since you were so careless about putting it in a public changing room. The back room would have sufficed, but you are intent on causing as much drama as possible. It is a wonder you were elected as head witch."

"How dare you," Lucinda spat.

Carnell's eyes flickered with red. "Me? You just told my granddaughter to fetch our members. She is not a fucking dog for you to order around. I keep asking her to contain her more aggressive instincts around you, but I am losing patience. I'm making the council aware of your bias toward her. If you and her end up in an altercation, she will have the support of most of this council. Be careful Lucinda. Demons and shifters can be unpredictable when provoked."

Lucinda touched her chest with her perfectly manicured hand. "She can't threaten me."

Carnell huffed. "She didn't. I did."

Reed walked into the chambers as Rhain entered through the portal. There was still no Fae representative, so the room was full except for Nishi. "Is there a problem?" Reed asked.

Carnell motioned to Lucinda. "She is upset that Faith has chamber access, as well as the ability to access shifter lands. She wants Faith to have a purple crystal. Faith needs to come and go without one of us needing to be here."

Reed shrugged. "Access to our land has nothing to do with the council. That is the alpha's call. Access to the council is Eve's decision as long as she is the shifter ambassador. She gave Faith access so she can continue to investigate the disappearances and find the missing tokens. Have you forgotten about the demon bounties she has had to deal with? I guarantee a demon took Nancy."

Reed's smile turned wicked as he looked at Lucinda. "Would you like to spearhead the investigation? It would require you to fight an unknown demon to rescue your friend. I'm sure it won't be as bad as the phoenix that almost killed Faith. Or the fury. Maybe you will get lucky, and it will be another flesh-eating empusa. I say we hold a vote on leaving Faith with a permanent crystal. Nishi has cast her vote by proxy."

Lucinda sat down and leaned toward Caton. "She is the bounty hunter. It's Saber's job to track demon criminals. She is one, after all, and can keep her crystal as long as she is working for the council." She had no choice in the matter, but I loved how she made it seem like she had made the decision. Bitch.

I wasn't sure if she meant I was a criminal or a demon, but if I caught her in a dark alley, the verdict could go either way.

Reed stepped onto the dais and took his seat. "It's settled then. What do we know about Nancy's abduction?"

"She wasn't taken from the store. There were no signs of a struggle. I was going to check out her home, but Greyson said it was unlikely she was taken from there. Does anyone have any idea where Nancy was last night?"

Carnell sat down in his council seat. "No, but I have an idea where the next site will be. I have narrowed down the scrolls and believe I have found the correct one. It's a ritual to raise a King of Hell."

He placed the scroll he had been holding in his hand on the table and rolled it out. He motioned me forward. I ascended the dais to look at the depiction on the thin, tan paper.

"What is that?" I asked, pointing to the starburst-looking crystal at the center of the depiction of a pentagram. It was identical to the one created by the demons I had come up against so far.

"That is the crystal the demons are creating. That is what it looks like when all the shards are assembled."

I pointed to the demonic runes. "Each pentagram had one of these symbols. How do you know where the rituals will take place? There are no coordinates on this… map. Or whatever that is."

Carnell tapped one of the points on the pentagram. "That is what threw me off at first, too. I assumed the final ritual needed to be in Ravenholde, so I was playing around with the locations you encountered the demons. They didn't make sense until you take all the locations into account with us at the center."

It clicked into place as I stared at the points. "If Ravenholde is the center, then three of the points are Williamsburg, Washington, and Wilmington."

He pointed to a dot on the scroll above the pentagram. "I am not sure what this is. There may be a sixth location. If there is an assembly ritual needed, that would take place after the shards were all created."

My forehead furrowed with my confusion. "But the map is not a perfect pentagram. How did you figure this out?"

He lifted one shoulder. "The ley lines. These sites have intersections. Ravenholde is the most powerful, which is why we reside here. The reason the gate was built here so long ago."

"Then if we ignore the random dot. The next ritual should take place at either Canton or Knoxville. Is there any way to narrow down the location within each city?" I asked.

Carnell shook his head. "The ley lines run beneath the entire town but are more concentrated at the center."

Reed rubbed his stubbled chin, and he stared at the map. "Why is a King of Hell trying to break your arrangement? I thought they were happy with the current accord."

Carnell leaned back in his chair but kept his eyes on the scroll.

"I don't think this is a current King. They all seemed quite upset about this development. I believe a high demon seeks to ascend to the position of King. That means one of the reigning Kings has to die. This is more than an assassination attempt. This would-be King wants to rule all of us."

Lucinda huffed. "Carnell, it is your job to keep the Underworld in line. Why hold a position of power if you are unable to accomplish this simple task?"

Carnell's growl was anything but human, and it was the first time he had displayed his more aggressive nature in front of me. "You are welcome to take my place, witch. The current Kings will chew you up and spit you out with only remnants of your soul left alive. Many of the sacrifices required for this position will not be to your liking, but I am sure you have the stomach for it."

"Are you insane?" Reed hissed at Lucinda. "Not a single council member is privy to the private accord Carnell made with the Kings to garner our safety. The council—hell, every single life in the human world is nothing without that truce. If he walked away, the gate would be unmonitored, and every type of demon could enter our realm."

Caton cleared his throat. "Lucinda spoke out of turn. She is just afraid for Nancy." He defended his plastic girlfriend, but not as vehemently as he had in the past. The warlock leader was beginning to regret his choices and crow looked good on him.

Carnell's eyes returned to their sea-green color as he took a calming breath. "Faith, I would try Knoxville. The ley lines are stronger there."

I nodded and took the crystal Greyson had given me out from under my black T-shirt. "You want to activate this thing?"

Caton tapped the table, and the magic board flared to life, showing a perfect map of Knoxville. "We will portal you to a remote location to ensure that you aren't seen when you appear."

I winked at Carnell. "Beam me up granddaddy."

Carnell's lip twitched as the white glow formed beside me.

CHAPTER 5

My boots crunched on the gravel beneath them. Air puffed on my cheeks as I exhaled, adjusting to instantaneous movement. Nausea and portal travel went together like flies on shit. Lucinda didn't want me to have access to the fastest mode of travel available. If things weren't so dire, she could keep her gut-wrenching magic. I'd be happier in the Corvette.

My stomach settled after a few moments, and I surveyed my surroundings. The parking lot was empty, with weeds growing through the cracked pavement. The building attached to it was boarded up and may have been a diner or some other kind of restaurant. The realty sign looked faded and in worse shape than the building it was attached to.

I made my way to the broken fence and the walkway behind the yellow building. Crushed takeout containers, used straws, and balled-up napkins confirmed my suspicions that it had been some form of restaurant back in the day. There were several black garbage bags full of trash and my unpleasant surroundings smelled of feces. But the sun was bright, making me thankful no one had seen me flash in.

The sound of rollers on the sidewalk made me turn as two teenage boys in black hoodies scooted by on their skateboards. Neither looked my way, so I continued to investigate the less-than-ideal location. There were no signs of a ritual or any nefarious activity. I jogged through the walkway behind the rundown building to find a food truck parked in the open lot next to it.

The smell of dark roast was heavy in the air. Inhaling deeply, I walked toward the silver truck where it originated. There was a flap open on one side and a menu board affixed to its side. The two boys with hoodies were at the counter ordering while two men in their forties, wearing white overalls with paint splotches, stood behind them waiting their turn.

It was unlikely there was a demonic ritual going on while the mundanes ordered coffee and donuts. I decided to grab a coffee and chat with the locals. If anything unusual had been going down, somebody around had to have heard about it. I got in line behind the two men and smiled when one turned around to look at me.

His nostrils flared as his blue eyes narrowed on me. The soft color was in contrast to his shaved head and athletic body. It was obvious he was used to hard work, as was his muscular blond partner.

"Hey, beautiful. I've never seen you at the Java Hut before," he said.

I took out my cell phone and hit the app for my GPS. "I have never been here before. Is the coffee good?"

He shrugged. "I have had better. There is a breakfast place a block down that serves the best coffee and pancakes you've ever had. I'd be happy to take you."

The speculation in his voice made me pause as his friend turned around. The blond was a bit younger than the bald man, but he inhaled deeply before he smiled at me. "Hey gorgeous. Sam isn't lying. The pancakes are next level at the Roast House."

While I wasn't new to being hit on, I wasn't at Club Bliss, and most guys didn't hit on you before your coffee if they wanted an actual chance of getting a date. Something was up. It was the twinkle in their eyes that alerted me to the succubus pheromone I was beginning to exude. Eve's suppressant had run its course. Shit! That wasn't good.

I glanced down when my phone beeped. "Thanks for the offer but I have to go."

Carnell's text alerted me the magic board had gone off. Crap on a stick. We had chosen the wrong location. I jogged through the walkway between the boarded-up building and the dilapidated fence, returning to the empty lot. I tapped my crystal after double-checking that no one was behind me. The portal formed, then I stepped through.

My stomach rolled as I stumbled into the council table. I grabbed the edge of the plant board making moss and leaves squish beneath my palm. "Just so we are clear. Portals suck."

I met Caton's eyes as Carnell stood. He took a deep breath. I glanced around the chambers to see if Rhain and Reed were still there. They were gone, but as Caton's eye flickered with interest, my stomach heaved.

"There is something I could give you to suck on," he said in a flirting tone.

Under any other circumstances, I would've pulled my saber and removed his head. I was well aware I was causing his interest. He straight up hated me, but he was looking at me like I was his favorite Snickers bar.

"I think I am going to be sick," I groaned.

Caton leaned forward. "I can take care of you," he purred.

Carnell pointed at the map. "You need to get to Canton, Ohio. The power surge was there. Make sure you take one of Eve's suppressants once you arrive. I will deal with… this."

His pheromone rolled off his skin like expensive musk. A second later, Lucinda grabbed Caton and started kissing him while trying to remove his shirt. I didn't envy my grandfather for the live show he was about to witness, but I appreciated him stepping in to save me from myself. I'd rather stick hot pokers in my eyes than have Caton look at me with interest again. Man, I felt like a turd. Caton was a prick, but he was also Eve's ex. She cared for him at some point even if I wouldn't go near him if he was the last man alive.

Carnell's pheromone filled my nostrils, making me wish Greyson was close by. I hadn't done it in the back seat of the car since I was twenty, but I would've had him on his back in seconds if he'd been here. Caton ripped Lucinda's shirt open, and I prayed eye bleach would remove the picture of her bare breasts from my mind as the white light formed beside me.

I should have thanked my grandfather for taking care of the sextivities I created at the council with my brief appearance. I was too busy darting through the portal like a chased rabbit. I fell to the ground as my stomach relieved itself of my breakfast wrap.

I choked in the fetal position as regurgitated egg and cheese dripped from my lips and landed on the grass beneath me. Puking up sausage wasn't nearly as bad as the mess I left my grandfather with. They didn't make a hallmark card to cover that shit and I hoped he forgave me. How did I explain this to Eve? So, hey. I dosed your ex till he hit on me. Also, thanks to my pheromone, he played hide the salami with Lucinda in the council chambers. Carnell was forced to watch their version of Sex du Soleil. Sure, that would go well. Not.

I pushed myself to a sitting position. It took me a moment to take stock of my surroundings. I used the gravestone next to me as a crutch to get to my feet before reading the inscription. The person had died more than twenty years ago, yet someone had placed the fresh daisies in front of the headstone in the last day or so.

The thick branches of the tree not far away shaded me from the overhead sun and hid me from the people in the distance, visiting their deceased loved ones. I hadn't had time to converse with Carnell and find out what had happened with the magic board, but if there was a surge of power, my next bounty had to be around here somewhere.

The cemetery was large, with wrought iron fences and a paved driveway winding between the graves. I could see a white chapel in the distance with stone angels sitting like sentinels in front of the entrance. While that would make an excellent spot to hold a funeral, it would not make a good spot for the ritual. Where would the demon hide in broad daylight?

The well-tended lawns with dried flowers and the occasional wreath dotting the rolling landscape held no sign of upheaval. Except for the chapel, everything was in the open. I couldn't understand why a demon would come here.

A squirrel chattered in the tree as if I were there to encroach on its territory. I pulled my hand from the cold headstone and turned in a semicircle until I noticed the string of mausoleums.

I jogged toward them, noticing the crack in the door on the one closest to me. There was a reason the portal had brought me here. I was fifty feet from the power fluctuation.

My stomach rolled as I leaned against the cement and peeked inside the dark room. There was a flicker from a candle inside. I had witnessed the scene enough times by now to know what was going on. I pushed on the door, surprised when it swung open enough so I could slide through the opening.

I kept my back against the wall as it took a moment for my eyes to adjust to the dark. I pressed so hard that my sword pressed into my spine. There was a reason I wore leather. How many abrasions would I have incurred over the years if I hadn't? It wasn't a question I wanted to answer, so I inched forward toward the light.

The low chanting started as I came closer to the pentagram with candles at each point. Nancy was gaged and whimpering. The noise she was making had covered the sound of my entry. The demon performing the ritual had pasty white skin and black lips. He had short fangs and appeared to have a human physique. He was naked but facing away from me as he pulled the shard from the bowl at the center of the pentagram.

I'd arrived too late to stop its creation, but I had a demon in a contained area and while I wasn't completely sure what species he was, I had been studying the texts Carnell bought from Odin and was guessing this guy was a templar demon.

They had some unique abilities, but they also had highly evolved sex drives. My current selection of sex-on-a-stick perfume would wrap pasty legs around my finger. I was suddenly glad I hadn't taken the potion Eve made for me.

I had never used my pheromone as a weapon, but I had been in enough fights lately to take a freebie. If I bagged this guy quick enough, I could get back to Ravenholde and call up my sexy warlock boyfriend for a roll in the hay. That was an idea I could get behind and the thought of Greyson naked increased the level of pheromone in the air.

I stepped away from the wall as the demon placed the shard against Nancy's chest. Her eyes flared when she noticed me. Unfortunately, she was immediately engulfed in a white light that was tinged with blue. There was no mistaking that portal and someone had access who shouldn't. The demon turned then and crooked his neck unnaturally to the side when he saw me. He inhaled deeply, but seemed confused by my appearance.

I smiled and crooked my finger. "Hey stud."

Yes, I was going to hell. Bounty hunter hooker was not a good look for me and I prayed I wasn't headlining for a B-movie on the adult channel as I approached him with a sway in my hips. I couldn't focus on the pasty skin of the demon before me, so I replayed images of Greyson with his shirt off. The pheromone was so thick in the air, I could smell myself. It took a lot of succubus spice for that to happen.

"Why are you here, succubus?" he asked with irritation in his voice. Weren't templars supposed to quiver at my feet with this amount of succubus spice in the air? He should be asking what my phone number is, not what I'm doing.

"Looking for you." That was true, but the activities on my dance card were different than he expected.

The demon moved closer to me. "You need to leave." He pointed to the door.

"I am happy to leave with you. Let's go outside. It's kind of stuffy in here."

His red eyes narrowed on me. "You wish to go outside to the cemetery?"

"Yeah, sounds like fun."

He motioned to the door. "I will follow you."

It took all my strength to turn my back and walk nonchalantly out of the mausoleum. I stopped just outside and smiled at him as he exited. "That's better. Now we can have some real fun."

His black tongue slid over his lips. "I doubt you would enjoy the same things I do, tri-bred. But I will kill you so you can host my children."

It took me a moment to realize he had played me. I had no idea why he wanted to be outside. He obviously knew who and what I was, so keeping me contained in a cement box seemed like a more prudent move. Since my pheromone had zero effect on him, he wasn't a templar demon.

I had no idea what he meant by hosting his children, and I didn't want to find out. "What are you?"

The demon smiled. "I am death. I am sure you have realized your pheromone does not work on my species. It will never work on a species that reproduces asexually."

I never read anything about demons that could reproduce without a mate. "That isn't possible."

My eyes fell on the area between his legs. I had assumed he was male, but there was no genitalia. He was neither male nor female and I had no idea what that made him. "Look. I didn't mean to offend you. I have never come across whatever you are."

"My species has been banned from this realm for thousands of years. That will change when the new King rises. Your carcasses will be fodder for my children, but you will be the first. It is quite an honor."

"I am going to have to pass on that." I stepped back as he hissed at me. There was a moment when you could tell you were under attack. While my opponent hadn't moved, he shifted his feet, moving his weight in preparation for an assault.

CHAPTER 6

There was a single crack beneath the earth, and I wondered if the demonic asshole hit a branch. I realized my mistake when the scraping started. The thumping of something kicking wood was a precursor to the scratching. I had a pretty good idea of what was happening beneath the earth, and I aimed my crossbow at the demon undead. He darted behind a gravestone and ducked down.

There was a massive cracking sound before the dirt above the grave caved in and ripples formed on the earth. A single hand punched through the ground before clutching the surrounding area. The zombie pulled itself from the depth of its grave, grasping the grass as it made its escape.

I noticed my demon peeking from behind the large gravestone. My attention went back to the woman clawing her way from her grave. She looked like she had been in her late twenties and her fancy dress had been a soft pink when she was buried. I hated what I had to do to her corpse, but she was coming for me. I had no doubt she was connected to the demon behind the tree. My crossbow made a tinging sound as I released the trigger and the resounding thunk as the arrow hit her in the head had her cheek falling to the earth immediately. I'd aimed for her skull hoping the lore about zombies was accurate. Score one for mundane myths.

This demon didn't care anything about the surrounding mundanes. There was no telling what they would think this strange attack was. Grave robbers that defiled their victims with arrows. The council needed to send a team back here to fix this disaster, but I needed to take the culprit who created this mess off the board.

Cracking sounds echoed around me, and I realized my demon foe was far more crafty than I gave him credit for. While I was busy with the woman, he had done something to cause more zombies to rise. I'd bet my next cup of coffee these were his children.

Dirt bubbled from five more graves that I could see. I had no doubt there were more. While I didn't know what this demon was, or how these things he created worked exactly, I could safely say he was definitely raising the dead somehow. I reasoned that killing him would deactivate the zombies, so I ignored the cracking sounds echoing around me and focused on my target.

He had ducked behind yet another headstone, and as I neared it I heard the familiar gagging sound. Why was he getting sick? My eyes widened as I watched him vomiting up a silver egg that burrowed beneath the ground the second it hit. He was hurling again, and his jaw opened, revealing a flash of silver in the back of his throat. I didn't wait for him to drop the second egg as I dashed to the side of the headstone with my crossbow drawn. He turned his head as I pressed the trigger.

I fell to my side as the arrow lodged in his skull. My aim had been true and had gone from one ear and out the other. The macabre sight reminded me of the time I had dressed up as a dead cowgirl for Halloween and had a fake arrow through the head. Luke and I had joked about me being an airhead all night. I wasn't laughing now.

My demon smiled at me before his pasty fingers with yellow claws wrapped around the arrow in his brain. He yanked it out as if it were no more harmless than the one I had worn for Halloween all those years ago. "You can not kill me tri-bred. You are not equipped to deal with a creature such as me." He released the arrow in his hands and dropped it to the dirt.

There was nothing in the books I had read about there being demons you couldn't kill. Or a demon that up-chuckled its eggs and planted them in dead bodies. This reality was far worse than any horror film I had ever watched. I had a brief moment of panic as five bodies rose from their graves.

While I knew how to kill the egg-infested corpses, I had a limited number of arrows. I wasn't prone to missing my targets, and six had always been more than enough. I'd wasted four already.

As the older lady in a floral dress lumbered toward me, I took her down with arrow number five. She reminded me of Mrs. Harriet and I cursed under my breath for the injustice placed on her living family if I didn't get someone with magic to sort this nightmare out.

There was a groaning sound from the next corpse, and in many ways, this was worse. The dead teenage boy was younger than my son and his skin was perfect, alerting me he had been buried recently. It was likely why he was able to create some vocal sounds. Albeit disturbing ones. He dropped to the earth as my arrow pierced his skull. But that left me with three more zombie attackers.

Two were older males that were ripening nicely, telling me they had been in the ground a while. The other was a woman in a stained yellow dress. With her thin frame and bald head, she had died recently of disease. I put my crossbow back in its scabbard and pulled out my saber. Stabbing things in the eye was not easy with a sword this size. I had my work cut out for me, literally, if I wanted to survive.

My demon foe proved to be far more intelligent than his pasty ass appeared. I was focused on the three undead lumbering toward me when two more grabbed me from behind. With the wind blowing toward me, their stench had been carried away from my location, but I got a face full of rotten meat when they attempted to bite my neck with rotting human teeth. I didn't pay close enough attention to the way my demon foe was moving his hands, but it was clear now that he was controlling his *children*.

I elbowed the older man in a blue suit, attempting to gnaw on me. The moment it took me to pull from his grasp was all my demon foe needed. He had proven he could direct his zombie minions, and while I took those few precious seconds to dislodge my attacker, he lunged from behind a gravestone.

I stepped back, but the tentative grasp the zombies had on my arms stalled my momentum and the demon's yellow claws scratched across my chest. I yelled as fire tore through my flesh. His claws felt like they were dipped in acid, and I brought my boot up and smashed down on one of my attackers.

He fell to the earth as I grabbed my saber and used all my strength to behead him. I elbowed another one as my demon foe ran away, using the trees for cover from the sun. I took two steps toward him, intending to follow, but my knees buckled beneath me. I had to add my latest foe to the list of demons to research.

The other three zombies turned to follow their master as I grabbed a healing potion from my jacket pocket. I downed the bitter liquid quickly before tapping my crystal. I had enough near-death experiences to know my body was not going to rebound from a single potion. My demon side would prevent my death, but only if I fed it what it wanted.

I swayed on my knees as the white light tinged with blue formed in front of me. "Home portal," I whispered as I fell toward the light.

My eyes flicked open. The portal had made me nauseous, but I had also passed out. I was lying on Carnell's lush, carpeted floor. Had the portal dropped me in his living room? Where was he located? I knew it was in his home, but I had never seen him use it. My eyelids drooped, and I felt my energy draining from my body like water through a sieve.

A rustling came from the library. I assumed Carnell was in there. "Carnell!" I yelled, attempting to push myself into a sitting position.

"Faith!" Eve said as she exited the library and ran to my side. "What happened?"

"I went looking for Nancy and I found the demon who took her. There is nothing like it in the texts I read. It upchucks eggs like the demon version of the Easter Bunny and hides them in dead bodies. I could kill the corpses, but not the demon itself. I needed to double down on my arrows for when I came at him again. Wait, what are you doing here?"

"Your grandfather let me use his library for research. He has information I haven't been able to find anywhere else." Eve backed away from me as her face flushed. "Oh, dear."

The smell of succubus spice filled my nostrils. "Dammit. You need to get out of here. I'm off-gassing pheromone like a cheap hooker on payday. I already dosed your ex and left my grandfather to deal with the fallout of that disaster."

Eve covered her nose with her sweater and took out her phone. "I have some of the suppressant potion. I was working on it for Carnell. Take it after you are… better. You can tell me about the Caton and Lucinda shit show later. I am texting Hunter. What do you need?"

God help me; this was embarrassing. I did appreciate that Eve was all business in a crisis. She had regained the backbone her ex-husband had so callously robbed her of while they were married. "Greyson." I fumbled to take my phone from my pocket. He picked up on the second ring.

"Hey, Faith. How is the hunt going?" His voice was upbeat and pleasant, making what I had to ask worse.

"Not well. I'm injured. I need you." My eyelids drooped.

"I will come to you. Where are you?" There was no embarrassment or anger in his voice. Only concern.

"I'm at Carnell's. Eve is here, but I have to send her out. I'm dosing her as we speak."

"Hunter will take care of her. I'm on my way." He hung up, and I met Eve's aroused and concerned eyes. "You have to go. He will be here soon."

"You're a mess. Do you have any more healing potions?" I could see what she was thinking on her beautiful face. She thought she was abandoning me while I felt like a total heel. Who did this to a friend?

"I already took it. Greyson is the only one who can help me. Go before it gets worse."

Eve dashed for the elevator when her phone chimed. I was sure it was Hunter, but I wasn't sure what I would say to the alpha the next time we met. Sorry I magically roofied your woman. I hope you didn't have plans for lunch. Yup, that was another good one. Not.

Seconds turned to minutes as I dozed with my cheek against the leopard print couch. My eye fluttered open when the elevator chimed.

CHAPTER 7

I could have cried when Carnell knelt down beside me. "Oh Faith. You need…"

"Greyson will be here any moment. Can you work downstairs for an hour?" It wasn't like my grandfather didn't understand what I was going through, but who asked their grandparent if they could borrow their place to have sex on the floor. My teenage years were less embarrassing than this.

"Of course. I'm glad you called him. Is Eve still here? You are emitting a serious amount of pheromone. She will be affected," he said.

It was then that I realized while his pheromone affected me, mine did not affect my grandfather. He explained the potency of the pheromone increased as the succubus or incubus aged.

"She was here. I dosed her before she left though, so I will have to deal with those consequences later. Right now, I can barely keep my eyes open, and I need to conserve my strength."

Carnell took out his phone. "Greyson just entered the building. I will go down and send him up." He was pragmatic, as if he weren't sending my boyfriend upstairs to magically rock my world. He went to the elevator, and the doors closed far too slowly.

When it chimed again, Greyson dashed from the lift and knelt beside me. His fingers went to the gashes on my chest. They were no longer bleeding thanks to Eve's healing potion, but blood had dried on my skin and the wounds were bubbled with pink lines of flesh, indicating they had recently healed. "What did this?"

"I don't know, but I am losing energy fast. I'm sorry for the short notice."

Greyson smiled before slipping my jacket from my shoulders. "You make it sound like some form of torture. Surely being with me is not that bad?" I was well aware he was teasing me to try and make me feel better and I appreciated it.

"You know, it's the highlight of my day. I was imagining being with you later, in your bed. My grandfather's floor isn't the sexiest of locations."

Greyson's eyes sparkled with arousal and if I didn't know they did the same thing without my pheromone affecting him, I would've felt bad. But knowing he wanted me when I was simply human had me sighing in relief as his lips touched mine.

"It's still nice to hear you say it." His lips moved to my cheek before he left a trail of fire beneath his soft lips.

I moaned, unable to hide my reaction to his sandalwood scent. My nipples peaked beneath my cotton bra and I arched toward his body. "I need you," I whispered.

"And I you," he said before he nibbled my ear.

Even his kisses were an aphrodisiac and sent energy streaming through my veins. Just the prospect of having him was a power boost. My hands went to his cotton shirt, and I unfastened the buttons quickly before slipping the material from his shoulders.

His skin was tanned perfection and if I wasn't recovering, I would've drooled at the sight of him. He pulled my shirt from my body and unfastened my bra. I was still wearing pants and my boots but he lay me on my back before removing them.

The lush carpet tickled my back as he tossed my clothes aside and removed his pants. He had discarded his loafers when he came in, but I hadn't noticed until he threw his jeans on top of them.

My tongue slipped over my lips in anticipation as he lay beside me and slid his hand down my side and rested it on my hip. He paused and pulled back so I could admire the chiseled features of his handsome face. He would never think so, but he was perfection in magically-charged skin.

Greyson smiled before nestling his head against my neck. "I don't want you to think my eagerness is because of your pheromone. I always want to be inside you."

His knuckles brushed the skin beneath my breasts, and my breath stuttered in my chest. He couldn't know how much his words meant to me. That this being his choice was more important to me than ever. With my energy returning due to my arousal, I intended to make the most of our midday retreat. My mistake was moving my hands over his sculpted body.

His muscles flexed beneath my fingers, and I focused on the velvet feel of his skin. His chest was drool worthy, and I lost myself in the silky touch of my fingertips as I caressed his nipple. A low moan vibrated in his throat as his lips moved over my neck. The air-conditioning within the penthouse blew against my skin but did nothing to calm the heat radiating from my flesh. We created an inferno together and while I had loved my first husband dearly, I had never felt anything like this. My body was an atomic bomb of desire waiting for my warlock to unleash it.

He kissed the indent at the base of my neck, then moved lower as I clutched his hair with my fingers. There was a good chance I was causing him pain, but I couldn't let him go. His arousal pressed against my stomach, alerting me he was just as desperate as I was, but he seemed in no rush to attend to his mounting desire as he pushed mine higher. Each flick of his tongue on my heated skin made my body quiver beneath his, and I whispered his name like a prayer.

His hand moved over my belly button before his mouth took possession of mine once again, fusing us together in an erotic tango. Static hummed in the air, and I could feel his magic swirling around us as if he had lost control of his immense power. The thought he was as addicted to me as I was to him inflamed me further and I deepened the kiss. This was desire on another level, and I froze as the realization that this man could hurt me filtered through my mind. Not physically, he would never do that, but I was already addicted to my warlock and if he ever tired of me, I would be lost. I had never had to rely on anyone in my life. Not even Luke.

"Relax, Faith," he whispered against my lips, as if he could read my thoughts. While his mouth continued to rob me of breath, his fingers moved over my breasts before cupping one in his palm. I moaned and arched against him, pushing closer to the muscled, perfect body that held me. My skin was ultra-sensitive, and electricity seemed to burst beneath areas he touched. I had always enjoyed sex, but never considered it could be this essential. Addictive. Like I could die if he wasn't connected to me. This was all that and more. And while he could walk away, I literally could die if he did.

His lips moved from my mouth, blazing a trail of fire to my chin and down the sensitive skin at my throat. His teeth nibbled as he moved to my collarbone and his tongue swirled over my skin. His hands stroked my sides in the lightest caress as he dipped his head to my breast. I moaned when he sucked an erect nipple into his mouth and my hands fisted in his hair.

His tongue flicked the hard bud before moving to its twin. The warmth of his breath heated my skin, making my legs move restlessly beneath him. As he moved lower, his hands cupped my breasts, pinching the nipples between his thumb and index finger as he continued his downward trajectory to my heated core. I begged him to hurry to reach his destination. Had I ever needed a man like this? I didn't think so, and that said a lot about my sexy warlock and the magic he created.

The mewing sound that escaped my lips was barely human. It wasn't demonic either. A picture of a cougar on the prowl filtered through my mind as Greyson settled between my legs and blew warm air against my aching pussy. If it was his intention to cool my heated core, he failed on a monumental scale. My body was on magical fire and Greyson was the only being alive who could quell the flames. My blood turned to liquid lava and sweat beaded on my brow as I clutched his hair. Several strands remained in my fingers as I tightened my grip. I felt like I was about to detonate as his soft lips whispered over my skin, leaving heat and desire in his wake.

I arced off the floor when his tongue took its first cursory lick of my sensitive lips. The pressure pressed my breasts against his palms. I searched for relief from the oncoming storm, but his exploration was intimate and endlessly slow. He took his time finding my most sensitive areas and lapping at me like a starving cat until I was chanting his name and begging him for release. I moved against his mouth in unabashed need.

His tongue dipped deep within me as his fingers massaged my clit with infinite slowness. He seemed content to feast on me forever and normally I would be happy to let him. My body ached for the release he was teasing me with. He drove my body higher and higher until I was panting for breath and praying to the god who had created him.

The erotic sensation started like a ripple in a pond, but turned into a thunderstorm of pleasure that spread over my body until I was clutching at him like an anchor in the thunderstorm. When I didn't think I could take anymore, his hands gripped me like a vise as he continued to feast on my body. I arched off the floor as a wildfire of sensation cascaded over me. Ripple after glorious ripple accentuated the effect until I was gasping for breath and clinging to his neck.

I took several seconds to get my breathing under control as he continued to kiss and swirl his tongue over my skin as if the very taste of me was addictive. He made his way up my body, pausing when he reached my breasts and wedged his legs between my thighs.

His full erection pressed against my slick entrance as he kissed his way up my neck and nibbled on my earlobe. My heartbeat began to pound in anticipation as he explored my body with his hands. His hands mapped every crevice as he continued tasting my skin. His muscles coiled beneath his velvet skin, and I knew his control had snapped.

He grabbed my hips with both hands and thrust deep inside me as my jaw opened in a silent scream. My core spasmed, and I clamped down on him as another orgasm ripped through my body like a thunderstorm. It continued like a ragging tsunami as his grip on me tightened.

"Dammit, Faith!" Greyson hissed. I liked him like this. On the edge and out of control. He continued to pump into me, and his thrusts were long and deep as he pumped through my orgasm and sent me skyrocketing toward another. His pace was relentless. I clutched his shoulders as if he were my only safe harbor. I needed this. I needed him, and my nails dug into his back as a growl of satisfaction escaped my lips. That was not demonic. That was a shifter marking her territory, but I filed the information away to dissect it when my body wasn't on fire.

"More," I pleaded as my body reached for another release.

I dug my fingernails into his shoulder, pulling him toward me with each delicious thrust. Fireworks burst behind my eyes before my body shuddered. He swelled inside me and whispered my name as I took him to paradise and clamped down on him when I came.

Greyson lay on top of me for some time before he garnered

the energy to slip to the side. "That was unexpected. Are you feeling better?"

I marveled at his perfection. With sweat beading his brow and upper chest, he had never been sexier. "I feel amazing, actually."

He smiled, and his eyes flicked with power. He pulled me closer to him. "Good."

"I don't know exactly what happened back in Canton, but thank you. I will try to give you more warning next time," I said.

"Don't apologize for wanting me. No matter the circumstances. Worst case scenario, we plan to have a sex marathon after every hunt."

I laughed. "You would have me bounty hunting on the daily."

He winked. "I would."

My gaze moved to the hallway that led to Carnell's library. The hall of orgies was in plain view from my vantage point, and my excitement drained from my body as I glanced around my surroundings.

CHAPTER 8

My eyes opened slowly as I snuggled closer to the warm body beside me. It took me a moment to realize I was lying on Carnell's carpet with a blanket over the top of me with my head on Greyson's chest. I remembered being cold and him grabbing a throw blanket from the couch.

My gaze moved to the large picture windows that gave us a perfect view of the city. The dark clouds rolled by slowly, oblivious to the world around them. The sun was falling in the sky, which meant it was about dinnertime. I had dozed off and Greyson had stayed with me. Holding me as I regenerated from my ordeal with the unnamed demon.

His consideration made me feel warm and fuzzy inside. I liked it more than I thought I would, but the reality that I was lying naked on my grandfather's floor sobered those emotions quickly. I leaned toward him and whispered in his ear. "Hey, stud."

Greyson's lips twitched before he opened his eyes. "Hey sex machine."

I tapped his chest playfully. "Ha ha. Get up. I think we dozed off. Carnell will be back soon."

"He came to check on you already. You were asleep, and he said to leave you. He went back to the club," Greyson said.

I rolled and grabbed my clothes in one fluid motion from the floor. "And the embarrassment never ends."

Greyson stood up slowly. "Your grandfather is the last person who is going to be concerned about something like this. I had already covered you with a blanket, if you are concerned with modesty."

I pulled my black T-shirt over my head. "It isn't just that. In the future, I would rather take one of the private rooms than fool around on the floor."

Greyson's eyes moved over me as I put my pants on and fastened the button. "You were in no condition to move downstairs. What happened to you?"

"I ran into a zombie demon that doesn't die and has venomous claws. The venom isn't really a surprise, but I have never seen or heard of anything like this thing."

Greyson put on his pants as the elevator pinged and Cal exited, wearing the robe he threw on when leaving the roof. His eyes moved over Greyson as my sexy warlock put his shirt on.

"I heard you were injured," Cal said.

"I wouldn't have instigated sexfest in Carnell's living room if I hadn't been."

Cal's eyes sparkled. "You worry about the strangest things, Faith. You are a succubus demon. Telling your species to refrain from sex is like telling a human not to eat."

I slipped my leather jacket on. "They go on diets all the time."

Cal shrugged. "Yes, but they don't want to."

I rubbed my forehead and turned to Greyson. "I am sorry about this."

Greyson's eyes flickered with blue power. "Honestly, I haven't had this much fun in years. You make every day an adventure, Faith."

Cal had a patch of gray on his chest, which meant he had left the roof a little earlier than he should have. His vibrant violet eyes almost glowed as they moved to the elevator. "Your grandfather is on his way up. Then you can tell us what happened."

I hadn't noticed the lift head down to the club. "I feel like a teenager getting caught with a boy in my room."

Greyson chuckled and slipped his hand to the small of my back. It was comforting to know I wasn't in this alone, but unlike me, he did not seem embarrassed. "I accept you for who you are, Faith. Besides, having your woman want you is not a hardship for most men."

Cal smiled. "You are good for her. She doesn't see the rare jewel she truly is."

I rolled my eyes as Carnell exited the elevator. His eyes went to mine immediately. "Faith, are you feeling better?" my grandfather asked.

"Yes, but I need information on the demon I came across in Canton. I originally thought it was a templar demon but, it's safe to say it wasn't. I was off-gassing pheromone like a brush fire gives off smoke and it was completely unaffected."

Carnell took a seat on the leopard-print couch before Cal sat on a faux-fur chair. "Tell me about this demon. If you believed it was a templar, then I'm guessing it had a humanoid shape and white skin."

I was too amped up to sit down. "Yes. It also had black lips and puked silver sacks out of its mouth. They solidified once the air hit them and burrowed into the ground. They reminded me of eggs. Since we were in a cemetery, they took over the corpses they found in the ground. It was like the zombie apocalypse. I could kill the demonic egg brains by stabbing them in the head, but when I put an arrow through the demon's head, he just pulled it out."

Carnell leaned forward. "You ran up against a bifron? I did not believe any demon would be so careless as to bring one here. They aren't trusted in the Underworld. They procreate by hosting the dead, and since there aren't a lot of corpses in the Underworld, they are more than willing to kill to get the carcass they need."

"What are those egg things?"

"Bifron reproduce asexually, but they take time to mature. The egg takes root in the brain of a corpse and the black filaments control all aspects of its host body. It slowly consumes the corpse and grows its own within the chest cavity. They can be killed by destroying the brain, but only until their demon body is fully formed. Then the only way to kill them after that is to incinerate their heart. That is far more difficult than you would believe. Its body heals from almost any injury and the ribcage is reinforced with thick bone not found in any other species."

"Yeah, I got the hard-to-kill part. What's the purpose? Why would anyone want that thing here?" I asked.

Carnell crossed his legs and put his knuckle to his lips. "Unleashing a bifron in our world is insanity. It could breed beyond our ability to cull it. A bifron is loyal to nobody. They have one instinct. Create more children. They are confined to a single island in the Underworld so they can't overpopulate. This is complete madness. I can't believe any demon would be so desperate and try to control a bifron. They will turn on their sponsor. It is only a matter of time."

I rubbed my hands on my pants. "They may be counting on me to kill it for them. There is no doubt the demon behind all this knows I am looking for them. But I don't care who unleashed it right now. It was obviously given a token to escape the Underworld and perform the ritual. The bifron created a shard before Nancy was portaled to its handler. It may be here to saturate our world with its demonic hatchlings, but it is doing another's bidding. At least for now. My only question is how to kill it? And if the eggs will die if I kill the momma demon."

"It's neither mother nor father. Rather both, but yes. The eggs need their parent until they mature. Like I said, killing the alpha bifron is not easy. You require a special weapon to cut through the outer layer and expose the heart."

"A special weapon?" My heart rate sped up, and I failed to keep my enthusiasm from my voice. Sharp toys were like catnip to me, and I never passed up a chance to play with a new one.

"There is a demonic hatchet that will cut the skin and bone surrounding the bifron's heart, but once exposed, you need fire. You do not possess magic, so I do not know what to suggest."

I turned and smiled sweetly at him. "I am going to see Odin to have him get me a flame thrower, then my man is going to magically boost its power and add it to my shrouded cache of weapons. No mundane needs to see me carry that around."

Greyson kissed my forehead. "Of course. I need to get your shield completed."

Carnell cocked his head to the side. "You have been working on that for a while. May I ask why it is not completed?"

Greyson's jaw tightened and for a second I thought he didn't like Carnell questioning him. "In order to create a magical shield for an individual, you need to tie the power to their essence. This is simple with a magic user. The cells at Scorchwood work in a similar manner, but each species has a specific resonance. A frequency in which to build the spell. Faith's tri-bred status makes her unique. I have not found a frequency that will bond with her yet. It is only a matter of time." As soon as he finished speaking, I knew he hadn't wanted to bring attention to the fact that I fit into no category.

Carnell nodded and looked away. "I see. Her heritage does make her unique, but it also makes her stronger in ways we have yet to explore. My apologies for insinuating you were not being diligent in your attempts. I know you are thorough in everything you do."

I stared at the carpet as the familiar feeling of being an outcast passed. "It hadn't been Carnell's intention to bring my freak-

to kill the bifron, I have to hit it in the chest and expose its heart before torching its ass with supercharged fire."

Carnell nodded. "Yes, but it will run if you are successful in cutting it with the ax. They are well aware this is the only weapon that can enable you to kill it."

I leaned the ax on my shoulder. "This day is looking up. Now how do I find this bifron? If it is anything like the other demons, it will not stay in the city it performed the ritual in."

Cal nodded. "You are correct. It will be on its way here if it is not here already."

"I figured as much. Since we have established a bifron has no reason to hang out at a club. Where am I going to find this thing?"

CHAPTER 9

Carnell shifted his weight on the leopard-print couch. He stretched his arm out and leaned to one side. "I wish I could give you more information. The reason there is no information on the bifron is anyone who attempted to study them died. I told you they are confined to an island in the Underworld. They kill their own in order to create their children when there is a shortage of dead bodies. It isn't just the insanity of allowing one topside that concerns me. I honestly don't know how another demon got near one on that island and was able to come to an agreement with one without ending up as a host for its eggs."

Cal's violet eyes focused on mine. "You should speak to Kormack. The empusa flesh eaters of the Underworld are reviled almost as much as the bifron. The empusa can't spread their infection though, so they are not segregated like the bifron species."

Greyson ran his hand down my back. "I have to get to the prison. Glinda is always finding new ways to disrupt her habitat. The warden is getting quite upset with her. She can be a lot to handle at times."

I kissed his cheek. "I bet. Go help the warden. Say hi to Brutus. I will be by with your newest addition to the prison soon."

His eyes flickered. "Be careful." He strode to the elevator as I turned back to Cal. "I need a flame thrower before I meet up with the undead puppet master again. Any idea what this guy's name is?"

Cal shook his head. "No, but it won't matter. They are all the same. Their need to procreate is their only driving force."

I went over and hugged Cal and he smiled at me, as if he had won something. Was I always so reticent with my affection? I moved over to Carnell, and he audibly sucked in a breath when I gave him a quick hug. The answer was yes. As I moved to the elevator and the doors closed, I thought I detected a tear on Carnell's eyelashes before he looked away.

I exited the elevator in the lobby to the chime and Dran waiting for me. "Carnell informed me you would be heading over to see Odin at the Bloody Bucket. Do you require assistance?"

I patted his cheek. "No. I can handle Odin. He is kinda sweet on me, so I pretty much get what I want from him."

"Of course, he is. You are an amazing woman," Dran said seriously. Man, my doppels were good for my ego.

"I left the Corvette on shifter lands. Can you get someone to retrieve it for Carnell? I need a new ride," I asked as we walked toward the rear alley.

"Yes. I took the liberty of gassing up one of the Mercedes for you and placing your weapons in the trunk." I tapped my back, completely forgetting I had arrived with my empty Bushel and saber. "Where did you get them from?"

"Carnell retrieved them from your suite when you were sleeping. He has refilled your arrows, but I recommend you get more from Odin. We only had six in inventory."

I jogged down the rear stairs after Dran opened the door, but he dashed in front of me to ensure he had my driver's side open before I reached the vehicle. "Such a gentleman." He winked after shutting the door.

The keys were lying on the console and I hit the start button before the high-performance engine roared to life. It was dusk now, which instilled the power Cal had to leave the roof when there were still some rays of light. The older a gargoyle was, the stronger and more powerful. Cal was the oldest member of his species and I had been blessed to consider him family. Not that I ever told him. I needed to change that.

The drive to the Bloody Bucket was short, and I was pulling up to Odin's sorry excuse for a truck in seconds. I slammed my door, and the door made a sickly chime as I entered. "I thought you were going to fix that thing. It sounds like a dying weasel."

Odin exited the back room, where he kept his dark magic artifacts and weapons. "I was planning to, but now that you said that, I am keeping it. I hate weasels." He tapped the front counter. "What can I get you, Saber? I hope it includes a roll in the hay. I'm in a bit of a dry spell."

I grunted. Honestly, I was getting used to being hit on because of my heritage, but it didn't make it any less annoying. "That wouldn't happen even if I didn't have a boyfriend. Keep your appendages to yourself."

Odin chuckled. "Lucky man. What do you need?"

My gaze roamed over the clothes racks and rifles mounted on the walls. The surplus store was unorganized, but it was the kind of place I would have frequented back in Cincinnati. My supplier back home didn't have a room full of dark magical objects, though. "A flame thrower."

Odin slapped the table and his eyes almost glowed, alerting me his wolf was just beneath the surface. I knew he was a hybrid, but I had no idea he had the ability to shift. Getting personal with the dark magic dealer was not an option, so I tramped down my curiosity.

"I swear you say stuff like that to get me hard." His voice was more than a little lecherous.

"You wish."

He smirked. "I do actually. But I have a problem of my own. Dagna is encroaching on my territory, and she has been increasingly difficult to find."

"I am aware of her exploits. What do you want from me?" I asked.

He looked me over slowly. "Dagna needs to be incarcerated. I would consider it a favor and am willing to compensate you for her incarceration. I wouldn't be upset if she didn't survive your meeting."

Capturing Dagna was on my bucket list, but I wasn't playing into Odin's hand. "I am looking for Nancy. The witch was abducted, and it may have to do with the location of the portal at her store. I am focused on the missing tokens and people, but if I come across her, I will shank her ass. She provided those nullifying coins to ensure Mina was abducted. I want to have a serious chat with her.

Odin rubbed his scruffy beard. "I would bet my left nut that Dagna provided the kidnapper with one of those coins to nab Nancy. That witch isn't as powerful as Lucinda, and she isn't as good in bed, but she knows her way around a spell."

While I wasn't surprised Odin had slept with both witches, I was surprised Nancy would take Lucinda's castoffs. I would rather bludgeon myself than date one of my friend's exes even if it was only a friends-with-benefits scenario. Odin didn't strike me as relationship material.

"I think she created a dark spell that shrouded a man who stole something from me. I am more than happy to apprehend her, but I have to stay on task. The missing people come first, as does the bifron, loose in Ravenholde."

Odin blinked several times. "No. It can't be a bifron. They are confined to a single island in the Underworld. Not even a King would risk a confrontation with those monsters."

"Someone did, and it's barfing up eggs like it's Easter. Now you know what the flame thrower is for."

Odin was a tough bugger, but he looked honestly afraid. "I will have it here for you by tomorrow morning. You need a special weapon to hold their skin open. They heal quickly, from what I hear."

"I have an ax. But I am curious how you know so much about the bifron. Even my grandfather had little information on them and there were no books on bifron in that set of encyclopedias you sold Carnell."

Odin opened his cash register and opened a roll of quarters before placing them on the tray. "They can't be studied. They kill everything they come in contact with... eventually. One bifron can start an apocalypse from what I read."

I made a mental note to see Odin in the future when it came to demons. He was far wiser about the Underworld than anyone realized. "Obviously, you have more reading material on demons. Make sure you sell Carnell those books when you are done reading them. I have no doubt you make copies. Do you know where this bifron will go next? We suspect he is on his way to Ravenholde, but have no idea about his habits."

"Other than creating more monsters, I have no idea what their habits are. I recommend you speak with Kormack. The flesh-eating empusa is the closest cousin to the bifron, but they are mild next to those undead up-chuckers. If you want to find this bifron, you should have Eve scry for him. She is the most powerful witch in town."

"Okay. Thanks. I was on my way to see Kormack, but wanted you working on the flamethrower. I will pop by Eve's first." I turned without another word and exited the store to the chime of a dying weasel.

Odin's suggestion killed two birds with one stone. I needed

more suppressant. My recent sexcapdes had strengthened me, but without a steady diet of the suppressant, I would be back at Greyson's door in hours.

I started the car and glanced at the streetlights as they glowed above my sunroof. The stores had begun to close, but some would stay open for another hour or so. Small-town life was predictable that way and I found I missed that. My tires crunched on the gravel as I pulled into the parking lot of Eve's store. The lights were on at the bottom and top, so she was home. I should have texted her before I left Odin's, but I had this sense of urgency. Everyone who had some knowledge of the bifron feared it more than any demon I had come up against. Considering how many monsters lived in the Underworld. That was saying a lot.

The door slammed on my Mercedes before I jogged up the steps to the entrance of the Blue Moon. I had zero magical ability, but I loved the store. The smells reminded me of fresh-cut grass and lilacs. Unlike Odin's door, Eve's chimed pleasantly as I entered, and she exited the massive kitchen she used to create her potions and wares.

"Faith. I wasn't expecting you. Is everything alright?"

"Yes, but I need more suppressant. That bifron took it out of me."

Eve's eyebrows scrunched together. "What is a bifron?"

I explained my encounter with the egg-laying demon and told her about the venom and how feared this particular demon was in the Underworld. "Yeah, so it sucks, to say the least."

Eve moved to the front door and flipped her sign to closed. "That is scary stuff. I have never heard of the Underworld segregating a demon species."

"Yeah, me either, and nobody has a ton of information on this thing. I am heading over to see Kormack after you scry for my bifron bounty." I placed my hands together in a praying motion.

Eve chuckled. "Of course. Come to the kitchen. I have everything we need there."

I followed her to the rear of the shop to the commercial kitchen. It was neatly organized with her supplies stocked in the cabinets. She got right to work. I admired her skills.

"How is Nishi doing?" I asked.

It was always hard when someone you cared about lost someone. Everyone dealt with grief differently and I never knew if I should stop by or give them space. I had always wanted the latter.

After Luke had died, I had withdrawn from the world. The only person I had made an effort for was Liam. My son still didn't know the truth about those events, and I prayed that my grandfather was wrong. That the potion that altered his perception of that night would last, and he never had to experience that nightmare again. I still woke beaded with sweat when that dream reoccurred. They were less frequent now, and I wondered if that too was due to my new relationship.

Eve sighed. "Not good. She still feels guilty for not loving him like he loved her. I think she needs time to come to terms with his death. Sadly, it won't be the last. The hunters have a dangerous job. To be honest, I almost feel this is Artemis preparing her."

I thought about her words. "That makes sense. It's tough, but when you are apprehending criminals, demons or humans, you are bound to take some losses."

Eve rolled a large map of Ravenholde out on the island she used to create her potions. I had seen her use it before and waited until she had the crystal moving in a circular pattern before I spoke. "Anything?"

Eve concentrated on the crystal. "No. Are you sure he is in Ravenholde?"

I thrummed my fingers on the counter. "No. He was in Canton this morning and I assumed he would be here by now. He could be anywhere since he has a friend with portal ability. Can you Scry for Dagna?"

Eve nodded, then did the same procedure before she sighed

and placed the crystal on the table. "I am sorry. Without something from either of them, I can only scry in a certain radius. I need their DNA to widen the search. Is there anything left of Dagna's at the old restaurant?"

I shook my head. "No. We took everything out before we started the renovations." My thoughts returned to Grayson before Glinda's face popped into my mind. My boyfriend was currently tweaking her cell. "Would her sister's hair work?"

Eve tapped her finger on her chin. "It likely would. I may get two signals unless the prison completely blocks Glinda. How will you get Glinda to cooperate? She is a lowlife, but I'm not sure she would betray her sister."

I smiled at Eve. "How sweet of you to think I was going to ask."

CHAPTER 10

*E*ve grabbed my wrist as I turned to leave. "You would need to be inside her cell to cut a piece of hair. She can use some magic within her enclosure and if they drop the walls to allow you to enter, everyone in there will be in danger."

The smell of lavender and mint waffled from the cauldron simmering in the industrial-sized kitchen. I had always found the mix of modern appliances with that one medieval one ironic and unusual.

"Grayson is at the prison. I promise not to do anything without him there. I am sure he can come up with a way for me to enter the cell unharmed. It's not like I will be staying to chat. I will get in and out. Promise."

Eve went to one of the cupboards and took out several vials. She placed them in a brown paper bag and handed them to me. "Here, take these. There are healing potions and enough suppressant to last you a few weeks, provided you aren't injured."

I took the potions. "Thanks. Add them to Carnell's tab."

Eve waved her hand negligently. "I just deduct it off what I owe him." There was a hitch to her voice I had noticed before when speaking about the money she owed my grandfather.

"Hey. You know, Carnell doesn't care about the money he lent you. Why are you concerned about it?"

Eve ran her hand through her dark hair. She was such a contradiction at times. Caton had destroyed her confidence when they were married, but when she was blasting hellfire bombs at demon foes, you would never notice the remnants of those insecurities.

"It isn't Carnell. I owe him so much. If he hadn't stepped in, I would have lost the Blue Moon and he didn't even want the money back. He would have given me the money and called it payment for saving him. He isn't the problem. I am."

"Why?" I asked.

Eve moved an errant strand of brown hair behind her ear. "I never did anything on my own when I was married to Caton. This was my only chance to build something on my own."

"But you originally owed that money to Ayesha. Correct?"

"Yes, but she was my friend, and we planned that loan. Carnell took over because he felt responsible for me and because…"

"You're my friend. Lots of businesses refinance, Eve. Switching to a different bank does not make the business any less yours."

Eve smiled at me. "That is a very mundane way of looking at things. But you're right and thank you. I have been feeling like I dodged a bullet instead of being grateful for the friendships I have made since my divorce." She hugged me and I patted her back awkwardly.

I released her. "I have to get to the prison, but I will text you as soon as I am free from the pocket realm and on my way back here."

"Sounds good. I will be here. Hunter is coming over in an hour. He is just finishing up some pack business."

I winked and strode out of the kitchen, then through the dim lights of the immaculate and inviting store. Eve had turned off the main lights, leaving only the display ones in the front window on.

I exited the Blue Moon and jogged down the steps to my Mercedes. It unlocked as soon as I put my hand on the handle, and I hit the push button start as soon as my butt was in the seat. The gravel crunched under my low-profile tires before I pulled out of the lot and was on my way to the prison when I realized I needed to make a quick stop.

The convenience store sign was unlit, and it had changed names so many times over the years I didn't really care what the current moniker was. I pulled into a parking stall beside the gas pumps and avoided the stacks of presto logs they were selling for indoor fireplaces. I passed the pallets of pink windshield fluid and headed for the door. It chimed as I entered and a teenager with a yellow and brown uniform nodded to me as I entered.

"Where is the beef jerky?" I asked.

He pointed to the last aisle. Though there were only four in the small store. "Chips, chocolate bars, and jerky are in that aisle."

I had to admire the young man's perception. There was never a day that chocolate didn't make better. I sauntered to the aisle before grabbing the last five bags of teriyaki jerky. Since he had made such a good suggestion, I grabbed two chocolate bars and a bag of corn chips. As I approached the counter with my arms bulging with junk food, I noticed the display case with thick hot dogs turning on rollers. "I will take a foot-long with the works."

The young man took tongs from behind the display case and assembled a hot dog, then added all the toppings the store provided, including sauerkraut. I paid with Carnell's unlimited-funds credit card, then took the bag of snacks in one hand and the hot dog in the other. It wasn't the fanciest of dinners, but I was used to eating on the fly and I needed my strength to deal with Glinda. Just the sight of her made me want to decapitate her. The warden was smart to relieve me of my weapons whenever I visited.

I got into the Mercedes and took a bite of my hot dog. It was surprisingly good for a convenience store, and I made a mental note to stop by again. It was on Danshire Street and close to the turnoff onto Scorchwood Lane. The location was perfect for my visits to Brutus. Yeah, I considered the pocket realm his. He was the shining light in that unusual place, and I prayed he wasn't the last of his kind, as my grandfather and Cal thought.

There was no traffic once I turned onto Scorchwood Lane. The mundane community thought the prison was a correctional facility, but they had no idea what kind of criminals it housed. It was a lie within the truth. Nobody was excited about visiting a jail and the long-term criminals had no friends.

There was a familiar rolling of my stomach as I passed the barrier between Ravenholde and the pocket realm, but it wasn't nearly as bad as it had been when I had first visited. I would need a few minutes to finish my hot dog, though. Regurgitated pork would not go well with the perfect black decor of my car.

I pulled into the roundabout and stopped in front of the plank gate that led to the prison. The crate where I would leave my weapons was already sitting at the entrance on the thick wood, but as I exited my vehicle, I felt the disturbance in the air and smiled.

Brutus shimmered beside me and his dinner-plate-sized pupils fixated on me with obvious excitement. I was the purveyor of snacks and no matter the animal, that moniker held me in high esteem. He sniffed at my door before I leaned over and grabbed the bag full of teriyaki jerky. I had tried several beef snacks, and this had turned out to be his favorite.

I ripped open the bag, but as I handed it to him, he nudged my side and didn't take the food I offered. "Since when do you turn down jerky?"

His nostrils sent a gust of air against my arm as he gently tried to nudge me away from my vehicle. I glanced at my foot long, minus a bite, assuming that it was the object of his curiosity. "Do you like hot dogs?"

His head jerked slightly, and I leaned in and grabbed the hot dog. As I pulled it from the vehicle, Brutus grabbed it from my hand with his scaled lips and backed away as if I was going to take it from him. "You can have it. I just thought you preferred jerky."

He flipped it into his mouth and made a sound similar to a purr, before cocking his head to the side and eying the bag of jerky in my hand. I motioned him forward with my fingers, and he leaned in and opened his mouth. I opened all five bags and dumped them in his open craw, before tapping his head. He swallowed the treat in one bite, then nudged me lovingly.

"To what do we owe the pleasure, Saber? I wasn't aware you planned to visit us today," the warden said from the front of the plank path.

I patted Brutus once more, then closed my door. "It wasn't planned. I need to see Glinda. Is Grayson here. I will need his help."

"He is currently boosting the efficiency of her cell. She finds new ways to disrupt her environment every time I turn around. I have never had such an unruly occupant in all my years."

The warden stopped before the crate as I placed my kubotan on it. The rest of my weapons were in the truck of my car, and I was about to walk forward when the warden cleared his throat excessively. It took me a minute to remember the small knife I had strapped to the inside of my boot. Cal had them specially made for me and gave them to me last week.

"Sorry." I withdrew the small shiv-like knife and placed it on the crate. "The rest of my weapons are in the trunk. I promise."

He nodded. "I am aware. Nobody can access your vehicle while you are on the premises. Come along." We walked a few steps before a faint odor reached our nostrils.

I pinched my nose, and the smell of rotting eggs surrounded us. "What is that?"

The warden turned and glanced back to where Brutus had been standing. "What did you give Brutus?"

"Beef jerky and a hot dog. You said dragons have titanium stomachs."

The warden pinched the bridge of his nose. "This hot dog. Did it have sauerkraut, by chance?"

"Yeah, why?"

"Sauerkraut makes Brutus... gassy. He loves it, but the prison occupants complain about the smell when he is given his favorite treat."

I paused before we reached the panel that allowed us access to the prison. "That was a dragon fart?"

The warden sighed as I burst into laughter. I didn't think I could love that dragon any more than I did. His harmless way of tormenting the prison inmates had just earned him a jar of the stuff. Maybe ten. I just had to get Greyson to reinforce Orek's cell. My favorite murmur demon was a victim of circumstance. Plus, I would never do that to his cat.

After allowing prison security to scan us, we entered the front door, and I smiled when I found Greyson waiting for me. "Hey."

He walked over and kissed my cheek. "This is a surprise. I wasn't aware you had business at the prison."

"Me either, but I need a lock of Glinda's hair so we can scry for Dagna. She had to have supplied one of her magic canceling coins to the bifron, and I am getting tired of her interference. I need to have a chat with her and find out who her contact is. She is working for the person who stole the tokens. I am sure of it."

Greyson glanced at the warden. "I can drop the wall for a few seconds without her knowledge. It would give you time to grab a sample of her hair, but I need the warden's authorization."

The warden shook his head. "Glinda is a witch. I cannot authorize this without Lucinda's approval."

I shrugged. "Call her and tell her I need it if she wants me to find Nancy. If she says no, tell her I walk away, and she can find her friend herself."

The warden walked over to one of the panels on the wall. He typed in a code I was sure bypassed the natural security system as I could never get a signal out of this place. Lucinda's face popped on the screen with her perfect red lipstick recently applied.

"What can I do for you, warden?" she asked with obvious disdain.

"Saber wishes to get a lock of hair from Glinda. She plans to use it to find Dagna."

"Faith has no right to violate a witch's cell. Regardless of her crimes."

I walked up to the screen. "No problem. A bifron took Nancy. They are some kind of undead demon that upchucks eggs and implants them in corpses. Good luck finding her. Let me know how it works out." I turned to walk away.

Lucinda's hand shot out. "Wait. Are you sure it was a bifron? Surely nobody would be so careless as to allow that demon in our realm."

As I met her gaze, I noticed the seeds of doubt and fear. She was actually afraid, which meant she knew exactly what a bifron was. "I went through half a dozen arrows, killing its zombie hatchlings, before it clawed me. So, yeah, I am sure of what it is. Fact of the matter is that we are fucked if it is allowed to remain topside for too long."

Lucinda paled. "A bifron cannot be allowed to breed. Take Glinda's hair and terminate that demon. I will have the council authorize a kill order. Do not capture the bifron. Kill it."

Normally, I would balk at Silicone Barbie giving me orders, but I actually liked this one. And I agreed with her directive. It must be my demon side. I wasn't this bloodthirsty normally, right? Sure, I could go with that. "No problem. I owe that bifron for ruining my favorite shirt."

Lucinda cut contact, and the panel went black. I smiled sweetly at the warden. "You heard her. Let's get a lock of Glinda's hair."

Greyson whispered in my ear, and I smiled at his tenacity. I thought I was rash, but my warlock had an ingenious way for me to get what I needed and avert any magical backlash.

"Keep that up and I will fall in love with you." The words fell from my mouth before I could censor them, but my warlock smirked before grabbing my hand and leading me to Glinda's cell. We passed Orek, but he was asleep in the corner with his cat Sasha curled in his arms.

Glinda looked up from the black leather-bound book she was reading, and her eyes twinkled with mirth when she saw me. "Faith, it's so good of you to visit."

"My friends call me Faith. You call me, Saber. If you ever get out of this cell, I will introduce you personally to my favorite weapon."

Glinda ran a hand through her gray hair. She wasn't glamored this time, and her skin creased around her mouth and over her eyes. "You are such a charmer, Faith."

Her eyes went to Greyson, and she made a kissing motion. "Hey handsome. Are we going to have another playdate soon? You know how much I enjoy your company."

"I have never been on a date with you, despite your many attempts prior to my marriage. You are a despicable representation of witches and warlocks alike."

Glinda's nostrils flared before she sat forward on her cot. "Is that so?"

She seemed distracted, as if she were concentrating on something we couldn't see.

I purposely banged my fist on her invisible wall. It made a sharp thud as it repelled my fist. "Tell me where Dagna is. I have had it with your sister."

Glinda's eyes widened. "While I have no love for my traitorous sister, she is family."

"I won't ask you again," I said.

Glinda's eyes sparkled, and I could tell she was enjoying herself. She placed her book on the side table beside her cot and rose from the bed. She moved till she was inches from me, but that force field would stop any altercation. She sniffed loudly. "Is that succubus spice I smell on Greyson? I can sense when it is used. How do you think I got the shifter Alpha to fall so hard for me? Dark magic dealers make a particularly potent version for shifter males."

"You bitch." I hissed.

She cackled as she put her hand to her chest. "Dosing a widower, though. Truly, Faith. That is something I would do."

"You would be surprised what I would do," I said coldly.

Glinda laughed until my fist connected with her face before I quickly grabbed a chunk of her gray hair. She screamed when I ripped it from her head and withdrew my hand. She blinked in disbelief before hitting the invisible shield that encased her. It made a loud thud and repelled her hand. "No! Faith, you will pay in ways you cannot imagine. So will your warlock lover."

"Unlikely. You are going to die in prison like a mangy dog. In pain and alone. But don't worry. I plan to find that rabid sister of yours and place her next to you. I'm all for a family reunion. I'm sentimental like that."

"How did you circumvent the ward?" she asked as her eyes flickered with power.

I smirked at her. "Greyson was kind enough to tell me that pain makes it difficult to focus your power. The shield was only down for two seconds. Looks like you missed your chance to escape."

The electrostatic charge vibrated around us as her cell went black and the prison shook. The warden glanced up at the lights above us as they swayed on their moorings.

"She should not be able to create such a disturbance," he said.

Greyson rubbed his chin. "She is getting stronger. It may be fortunate that Faith assaulted her. I need to strengthen the ward of her cell more than I realized. She pulls three times the power of any other inmate as it is, but she isn't diminished as she should be."

I held up the lock of gray hair. "Why does assaulting Glinda make me so happy?"

The warden cleared his throat. "Most likely because you are part demon, but that was uncalled for. We do not cause our inmates harm."

My eyes narrowed on him. "She killed so many innocents and you are worried about a punch to the face? I didn't even hit her that hard. Just enough to surprise her. She didn't even bleed."

Greyson touched the black cell. "She summoned dark magic. She planned to kill you."

I shrugged. "Shocker." I touched his arm. "Thanks for your help, but I have to go. Eve needs this to find Dagna."

CHAPTER 11

Moonlight filtered above the trees as I turned off Scorchwood Lane into Danshire. The traffic was light and in minutes I was pulling into Eve's parking lot. The lights in the front window illuminated the display behind them, but the lights in the store were dimmed. Since the lights upstairs were off, now, I was sure Eve was in her Kitchen. Likely making more potions.

I turned off my engine and jogged up the steps to the door. It chimed as I entered. Eve had left it unlocked despite being closed for the day to her regular customers. That could be dangerous, given what had happened lately. Eve exited the lit-up kitchen door.

"We are back here," she said, while smoothing her hands on her black apron with the store logo on the front.

I entered the industrial kitchen to the smell of mint and strawberries. "That smells good enough to eat."

Eve chuckled. "I wouldn't recommend it. That is a foot lotion."

Hunter smiled as he leaned against the sink area. The alpha

was attractive and muscular, but he possessed a sadness and wisdom his pack mates lacked. Maybe it was just the atrocities Glinda unleashed on his pack or the traits that made an alpha unique. Despite my heritage, I didn't know enough about pack life to determine the answer.

"Did you convince Glinda to give you a piece of her hair? Eve told me that you plan to use it to find Dagna. I just can't see her helping you."

I shrugged and my leather jacket creaked a little. "She says she has no love loss for her sister, and she wouldn't help me." I placed the hair on the island. "Not like I would let that troll stop me."

Hunter's growl was low, and Eve and I both froze. He cleared his throat. "I am sorry. That isn't a smell I thought I would experience again. The memories that conjures are not pleasant. Faith, will you tell me how you got this from her? I know you couldn't enter her cell and if she didn't offer it through the cubicle…"

"If I tell you. Do you promise to associate this lock of hair with the story?"

Hunter arched an eyebrow as he crossed his arms. "Sure."

"Greyson was there. She was inappropriately flirting and trash talking, of course. I arranged to have him drop her cell wall for a couple of seconds. He warned me it's harder for a witch or warlock to focus their power when they are in pain. So, I punched her in the face and yanked the hair from her head."

Eve put the herbs in her hand on the counter. "You did what?"

Hunter put his hand over his mouth, but his laughter escaped before his eyes sparkled and he met my gaze. "Faith, you have literally made my day. Thank you for that."

I made my best impression of an awkward curtsy. "You know I aim to please."

Eve slapped Hunter's chest playfully. "Hunter, don't encourage her. Lucinda will crucify her for this, and Greyson could get into trouble for helping her."

I sauntered over to the island and grabbed one of the chocolate chip cookies sitting on a plate. "Not true. The warden would not let me take her hair without consent, unless Lucinda gave permission. Bimbo Barbie was her usual charming self until I told her to fight the bifron herself and find her friend. I didn't think that plastic witch had a decent brain cell in her head, but she was afraid of a bifron. Needless to say, she authorized my incursion in Glinda's cell."

Hunter dropped his arms, and the muscles flexed in his arms. "The warden allowed you to assault Glinda?"

I cleared my throat. "Not exactly. I didn't tell him what I had planned. He is a little incensed that I… assaulted her. I may have to avoid the prison for a while. Then there was the Brutus thing."

Eve turned to me. "Something happened to Brutus?"

"No. I gave him a hot dog with sauerkraut. Apparently it makes Brutus gassy. The prison realm is currently experiencing air-quality issues."

Eve pursed her lips and glanced at Hunter before they both burst out laughing. Hunter composed himself quicker than Eve.

"You managed all that in under an hour? You are a force. I will give you that," Hunter said.

Eve approached the island and picked up the lock of hair. "You are terrible, but I have to say she had it coming. She must have been pissed when she realized you dropped the cell walls, and she missed a chance to escape."

"Oh yeah. She tried to use dark magic on me. It shook the entire prison. Greyson is modifying her cell."

Hunter's eyes flashed with those of his wolf. "That sounds like Glinda. I am of two minds about her escaping. My wolf has wanted to hunt her since the betrayal of my previous alpha was discovered."

I wanted to keep my species' involvement in Glinda's deception from hurting Hunter further, but I wouldn't allow dishonesty between us. He was in Eve's life for good, and that meant he was in mine. "She told me she used succubus spice to keep the alpha addicted to her. I'm sorry, but he never stood a chance."

Hunter nodded. "She used several additive agents and magic to enthrall him. But we investigated those potions and how they were created. A succubus or incubus was killed to create that dark potion. Your species had nothing to do with it. It took magic to create what was wrought."

Eve focused on wrapping the strands of hair around the crystal she used to scry, but her eyes were haunted. Hunter swore under his breath and moved to her side. He placed his hand on her back. "Everything Glinda did was on her. It was wrong of us to hate every witch because of her actions. I'm sorry for the careless comment."

Eve kissed his cheek quickly, then continued to wrap the hair. "It's okay. Witches are people. We have our good ones and bad ones. Lucinda isn't exactly a shining star of reputability either."

I grabbed another cookie. "I agree, but she gave me the kill order for the bifron."

"I'm not surprised. That thing sounds like a nightmare," Hunter said.

I chewed the chocolaty goodness. "Worse."

Eve finished attaching Glinda's hair to the crystal. She placed it on the counter and positioned her map on the island before holding the crystal above it. She spoke the spell to start the crystal, moving in a circular motion. "The wards around Scorchwood should prevent the crystal from picking up Glinda. Let's hope her tie to her sister is close enough to get a reading."

The crystal stopped in midair and pointed in a straight line to a green block on the map. I glanced at the location, unsure it had worked. "That can't be right."

She touched the crystal, and it went slack. "She is at the hospital. It's a large place. I have no idea where she could hide."

I thought about her setup at my currently under-construction store. "I do. She is in the basement. She is smarter than she looks. Nobody would have looked there for her."

"Do you need backup? I can go with you while Eve finishes up her work. They are ruined if she stops in the middle of their creation."

"It's just foot lotion. I can make more," Eve said.

I popped the rest of my cookie in my mouth and grabbed two more from the plate. "She is likely alone and feeling safe. I will call if I need backup." I held up the cookies I had just snatched. "Thanks for dinner."

"That isn't dinner," Eve grumbled as I walked toward the dimly-lit store.

I chuckled as I exited the Blue Moon and got into my Mercedes. The hospital was in the mundane area and on the other side of town. Fortunately, it didn't take more than twenty minutes to get from one side of Ravenholde to the other, and Eve's store had more of a central location.

The engine roared as I pressed the ignition, and I was pulling from her parking lot in seconds. I preferred to avoid traffic, and the hospital would always have an influx of patrons, so I took a few side streets that took me through the quiet streets full of single-family homes where the mundanes lived. Their houses looked similar to the supernatural community with manicured lawns and paved driveways; the colors differed, as did the landscaping. It was obvious they took pride in their homes. I turned onto a roundabout that led to the parking lot behind the emergency entrance of the trauma center.

I parked next to a brown station wagon that had more rust spots than my first car, then got out and opened my trunk. I glanced around the large lot before taking off my jacket and slipping my saber onto my back. There was a secure feeling to having it balanced between my shoulder blades before I put my leather back on.

My fingers slipped into my kubotan key chain. I flipped the

keys in a circle around the ring as I strolled toward the rear entrance of the hospital. It was labeled outpatient on this side, but I knew the maze of departments contained within.

While I hadn't been to that hospital since I was a child and my mother brought me to assess a suspected broken arm, it had turned out to be a sprain and I had healed within a couple of days. Too fast for a mundane, but I hadn't realized that at the time.

An orderly was wheeling an elderly man in a hospital wheelchair to a blue sedan parked in front of the entrance when I neared the door. Their exit had left it open for me, and I jogged through the doors before they closed. I passed a nurse talking to a young couple in the hall before I cleared my throat of the smell of antiseptic. I had always hated the smell of hospitals. They always reminded me of decay and bleach.

I passed two doors with numbers on them before one that was marked the utility room. It also had a red plaque that said Employees Only, but that was exactly what I was looking for. If this hospital was like the others I had been forced to chase bounties into, there was an array of power supply and service rooms beneath, where an enterprising witch could hide out.

I pushed the bar of the heavy metal door before slipping through and down the cement steps. The bottom was a large room with power supplies and massive pipes. There was a hallway that led to another section of the hospital, and I started to follow the steel pipes mounted on the ceiling until I heard a sound.

I turned as Dagna seemed to appear from nowhere. "You have a bad habit of showing up when I least expect you," Dagna said with a smirk. She looked pleased to see me, which put every nerve in my body on high alert.

My fingers tightened on my kubotan. "Yeah, I'm like a bad penny. I keep turning up."

Dagna cackled as if I had told the funniest joke she'd ever

heard. Her gray hair hung in thick strands as if she hadn't had a shower in years and her clothes were dirtier than the last time I saw her. All in all, she looked like a warm dump. "You have pissed off some powerful people in the Underworld, Faith. Someone has commissioned your death."

As a bounty hunter, I had learned long ago you were doing something wrong if you weren't pissing somebody off. Those individuals were always on the wrong side of the law. "Death threats are so five minutes ago. How about you show me instead of telling me?" I motioned her to approach. "Come on Dagna. Don't be shy."

Dagna sneered and her yellow rotting teeth bit into her lower lip. "You will die tri-bred." Her arm shot up and lightning formed on her hand before she released the magic and it arced toward me.

Having fought with Eve on multiple occasions and seen how fast and effective her hellfire was, this parlor trick seemed like a pathetic attempt to mimic my powerful friend. I lunged out of the way easily and stopped her from moving to the corner.

I glanced around, but the only thing in the room was a basketball lying on the ground by the wall. "Is that supposed to frighten me? If you were any slower, I would have time for a smoke before that bolt hit me."

Dagna hissed, and spittle leaked from the corner of her mouth. "You have no idea what is coming."

I shrugged. "Enlighten me. Are you working for Rerek, the demon who stole the tokens, or do you have your own agenda? Tell me how you contacted the bifron. Who let it topside? Where is Nancy?"

Dagna waved her arm erratically. "So many questions. Wouldn't you rather know about the shadow creature? That was some of my best work. To create that for a non-magic user was a stroke of genius. It was some of my best work."

I had not forgotten about the loss of the shard. The bitch had just confirmed she was responsible for it. "Who was in that shadow shroud?"

Dagna's eyes glinted with speculation. "It's genius, isn't it? That could have been a family member or friend and you would never know it."

Was she insinuating the shadow creature was someone I trusted? A family member. A friend? Or was she just messing with me because she was a sad, pathetic creature who got off on other people's pain? Sadly, it could be all those things or none of them. "Who did you make that thing for?"

Doubt was a bitter pill, and my doubt allowed Dagna to dart to the corner of the room. She kicked the basketball at me, and I almost sighed before catching it. If dodgeball was an Olympic sport, I would have had a gold medal. I loved that game. My smile died when hers widened.

Dagna snapped her fingers, and the exterior of the basketball dissolved in my hands. I stared at the glowing orb as if it were an alien. In truth, I had no idea what I was holding. It pulsed beneath my fingers as Dagna cackled. "Stay very still, Faith. If you drop that bomb, it will take this entire building down. So many innocent lives at stake." She turned to leave.

"Don't you dare walk out of this building," I snapped.

Dagna smiled. "And what do you plan to do? Allow hundreds of mundane innocents to die so you can seek revenge?"

"You bitch."

Dagna touched her lips coyly. "Sweet talker. I would say see you next time, but eventually you will get tired and once that orb hits the ground and the outer shell is breached, this hospital will be a hole in the ground." She walked away as I weighed my options.

Her footsteps echoed as she ascended the steps, and I flinched when the heavy door slammed behind her. I had no idea if she could detonate this thing remotely, and I didn't want to find out.

I lifted my arm, so my pocket was closer to my face while keeping my grip on the orb. "Call Eve."

The sound was muffled as it rang, but Eve picked up immediately. "Was Dagna at the hospital? Do you need backup?"

"Yes to both, but she escaped, leaving me holding an atomic bomb."

CHAPTER 12

It took me a few minutes to figure out why I was dizzy. The orb seemed to suck the energy right out of me, and I was pretty sure if I had been human, I would already have dropped to the floor. My temples throbbed as pain radiated in my skull. It had been years since I had a migraine. That bitch was going to pay for making my temples feel like they had a jackhammer inside, while my stomach flipped like a fish out of water.

I swayed on my feet before Eve's voice echoed around the room and she rushed down the steps. Her gaze moved around the space as she set down the large black bag she brought with her. She was wearing the same cream sweater and blue jeans she had on in the store, but she had removed her apron. "Where is Hunter?"

"He alerted the police there was a bomb threat. They are quietly removing the people that are safe to travel."

I tipped my chin toward the glowing orb. "Do you know what this thing is?"

Eve circled around me with her eyes on the pulsing globe. "No. I have never seen anything like this, but I called Grayson. He will be here in a moment. You just need to stay still."

"Okay," I whispered.

My eyes closed before Eve grabbed my shoulder. "That's easier said than done. You look like you are about to pass out?"

"The orb is sucking my energy from me. I haven't felt this nauseous since my first trimester of pregnancy."

"Don't throw up. If you drop that thing, we are dead. If Dagna was as cocky as you said, then she wasn't lying about this thing hitting atomic proportions."

"Trust me, I believe her."

Eve held her hands over the orb, and I felt a slight wave of energy go through me. "Damn."

"What is it?" I asked, not really wanting the answer.

Eve tapped her knuckle on her lip. "It's like a magical Rubik's cube with a plutonium center. I can't deactivate the bomb without getting through the layers of protection she placed around it. It's sad, but I have to admire her ingenuity. It's unfortunate she turned dark. This magic is brilliant."

Of course, the dark witch had to be smart. I wouldn't have fallen for her trap otherwise. Still, she couldn't have known I would find her here. She may have had that bomb here for anyone who tried to stop her, or she had planned to bring this building down by using a human. None of the scenarios were good, and I was relieved I had intercepted the orb before she killed hundreds of people.

"Can you start working on the outer protections? I need this thing deactivated soon. I'm not lying when I say I am asleep on my feet."

Eve placed her hands over mine and her eyes flickered with blue fire as she concentrated on the orb. It pulsed brightly before she snatched her hands away. "Dagna is smart. This has a double latch system. One protection spell was layered with another. It takes two empowered individuals to release the wards. They have to work in tandem."

"Wouldn't that mean that it took two witches to create those protection layers?"

Eve nodded. "Dagna has a partner and if I was a betting woman, I would say it is Glinda. There is little difference between the magics. They seem identical. Every magic user has a signature, and these are too close not to be related."

"Glinda has been in prison for years. She couldn't have helped Dagna create this," I said.

Eve shook her head. "This orb was inert until she activated it. The orb could have been created twenty years ago. Like an engine that hasn't been turned on. Dagna activated it now, but I think she and Glinda created this orb bomb a long time ago."

"Shit. Do you think there are more of them?"

"No idea. This is dark magic, and I never dabbled in this. Not even a little."

"Well, I am thankful for that. Greyson won't know either, will he?" The thought that neither of my powerful empowered friends could help me had never occurred to me until Eve glanced uneasily at the stairs. The sound of footsteps echoing through the cement room with steel piping pulled me from the dark thoughts as Greyson approached us with smoldering eyes.

Usually, I got that look when we were in the throes of passion, but this was a fire of a different kind. My warlock was straight up furious and, as his eyes fixated on the orb in my hands, the hairs on my arms stood up. He was radiating energy like a Duracell.

"How do we deactivate the bomb?"

Eve pointed to the center of the orb without touching its surface. "There is plutonium at the center. The protection wards have to be unlinked simultaneously or it will detonate. I didn't want to try without you. How is Hunter doing with the evacuation?"

"He called Faith's detective friend. Bracken is helping coordinate, but we only have so much time before their bomb squad arrives. Fortunately, they only have one specialist in town, and I ensured he wasn't answering his cell."

"You didn't hurt him, I hope."

"Of course not. He worked a ten-hour shift and is asleep. I ensured his tech was offline. He is a good man who helps with multiple projects in town. His bomb skills are rarely used, which is why he left the react team in Cincinnati and moved here. He is older but the only specialist on the human police force."

I staggered, but managed to stay upright when Greyson grabbed my shoulder. "Sorry."

"You can't break contact with the surface, or it will detonate. An interlocking orb makes an effective protection."

Eve frowned. "An interlocking protection isn't dark magic. This is."

Greyson nodded. "Dagna infused the orb with a siphoning spell. It is sapping Faith's energy. She was careful to have the spell stop once the subject of her attack is asleep, but in this case, that means the bomb falls from Faith's hands and this hospital turns to rubble."

"Could I walk out? Even if we can't deactivate it, I don't want anyone else to die. We need to get me to a remote location."

A tear formed on Eve's eyelashes. "You are not doing this to me. We just lost Nathan."

Greyson touched my shoulder. "That isn't an option, but it wouldn't work. The more energy you use the quicker the orb drains you. The only way this block isn't destroyed is if Eve and I unlock the interlocking wards and destroy the plutonium core."

Eve leaned closer to the orb. "How do you know so much about dark magic? I have connected with you many times when we work together. You have no traces of it."

Greyson stared at the pulsing orb. "Those in my position with the council study dark magic, but we do not use it. I must combat its effects daily at the prison. Glinda keeps me on my toes when it comes to the dark arts and how to combat its uses."

Eve pointed to the right side of the globe. "Do you see where the threads of magic connect to one another? If we disconnect each side at the same time, it should remove the first layer."

Greyson walked around me. "Yes, but they have to be snapped at the precise moment, or the magic will recoil like a rubber band. She has tethered it to the next layer. The threads are moving like a loom, and we have to wait till they are slack before we disconnect them."

As I listened to their strategies on how to unlock the magical death orb, I understood how dire my situation truly was. I had to hold on till they evacuated the building, but there was one thing I needed to do before I told my friends it was time for them to leave.

"Eve, can you take my cell phone out and place it on speaker? You two do what you need to. I want to talk to my son."

Eve gave Greyson a hard look, but did as I asked. Both knew why I was calling my only son. They would have done the same thing in my shoes. Eve placed the phone at my feet and clicked Liam's contact before hitting the speaker.

"Hey Mom," he said.

"Hey babe. How are things?"

"It's madness. It's like half the city went to crazy town. We have thirteen active bounties. Max says we will need to hire another bounty hunter. Sorry, I can't handle it all on my own."

The note in his voice alerted me he felt he was letting me down. I had handled that many bounties on my own, but I had years in the business before I was that effective. "Honey. That is great news. All businesses have to expand. Max was able to help me in the field when we started. He just can't do that for you. I am glad you are putting his safety above our bottom line. If we are that busy, we can't take on more clients without someone else."

"Thanks Mom. I wasn't sure you wanted another hunter."

Greyson gave Eve a look and that let me know they wanted to start on the orb.

"I just wanted to tell you that I love you and that I am proud of you. Take care of Max, okay?"

"Always do. Listen, Max is hoping you will do some training once we hire. We could send the newbie to you for a few days if you like?"

"Yeah. I will talk to Max about it later."

"Okay. Love you, Mom." He hung up as my chest heaved.

Greyson and Eve stood on either side of me. There was an electrostatic charge as they silently focused on the pulsing orb in my hands.

There was a sizzling sound as steam rose from the orb, and it shrunk in size. "What was that?" I asked.

"We released the first protection. We have to wait until the threads go slack again to unfasten the next one. They move at different intervals on each layer. We have to get the timing right or things go wrong."

My eyes drooped before Greyson spoke.

"Eve, we have to wait a minute. I have something that may help, Faith. Her strength is waning too quickly." He slipped his hand into his pocket and pulled out a gold chain. The smooth finish on one side had symbols I didn't recognize carved into the surface. It was unique and beautiful.

"What is that?" I asked, as he gently fastened it to my wrist.

"It's a location charm. If you are ever in trouble or need immediate assistance, simply run your fingers over the runes. It will send me a signal to come to your aid."

"I am impressed you had time to make this on the way over," I teased.

He smiled wanly. "I have been working on it for a while. Honestly, I was waiting for the right time to give it to you."

I winked. "Every girl needs a good magical alert bracelet."

Greyson grabbed his phone and checked it when it chimed. "Hunter says there is no way to move the mundanes in time."

My heart hammered in my chest. "You have to do something. Please don't let my stupidity get these people killed."

"You didn't do anything wrong, Faith," Greyson assured me.

"I saw the basketball in the corner. It was obvious Dagna was trying to get to it. I didn't recognize it as a weapon."

Eve huffed. "Like anyone could predict a magical bomb inside a ball." Her eyes roamed around the cement room. "This place is a fortress. If we created a shield, we could reinforce the room. There would still be structural damage, but if we kept the blast contained, then nobody would die." I hated that she meant everyone except the three of us within the blast radius.

Greyson nodded. "I can pull from the prison grid for a few moments. I will create the ward. It will essentially be a pocket realm within this room, but it won't last long."

"It doesn't have to. Only long enough to allow us time to disengage the locks between layers on the orb."

Greyson moved his hand in an arc, and a bubble formed around us. It wasn't invisible like the one surrounding the prison, but my nausea increased, and I blew out a quick breath. "It's done. We need to work quickly. It won't take Glinda long to discover a weakness in the prison wards. She is relentless in her attempts to escape."

Eve and Greyson focused on the orb without another word. There was another power surge accompanied by a sizzling sound before the glowing circle shrank. "That last layer isn't an interlocking protection."

"No. It's an usurping spell. The Fade sisters created this for a witch. It wasn't meant for a non-magic user."

I glanced between them. "What does that mean?"

Eve motioned to the orb. "The last ward forces the person touching it to sacrifice their magic in order to unlock the ward. It can only be done by the person holding the orb."

"But I don't have any magic."

Eve smiled. "Exactly. Tell the orb you are willing to make the sacrifice."

"I am willing to make the sacrifice," I said.

The orb pulsed before its light dimmed. In seconds, it looked like a silver ball, but it held no weight.

"Tell me I am not holding onto plutonium?"

"You aren't. It's still inside the casing, but the bomb is inert. Greyson should take it to the prison. It isn't safe in the community."

As soon as the orb's light dimmed, the energy that was being sucked from my body halted. Unfortunately, it wasn't replaced and as soon as I realized I wasn't about to detonate, my legs crumbled.

Greyson caught me as Eve grabbed the orb from my hands. "Let's not do that again, shall we?" he said as he held me against his body.

"Yeah, that sucked hind tit."

He chuckled and kissed my forehead as I slowly got my feet underneath me. The surrounding bubble dissolved, and I was glad the power was returned to the prison. But my relief was short-lived when Greyson's phone blared with a siren sound. "Shit. I have to go. There has been a problem with Glinda's cell. If I don't return and stabilize the power flow, it could have dangerous effects on the entire habitat."

I hugged him. "Thank you for coming to my rescue. I'm fine. You go."

He turned to Eve. "She won't leave her car here. Will you follow her home and ensure she goes to bed?"

Eve folded her arms, enjoying she had just been assigned my personal warden. "Absolutely."

CHAPTER 13

I took a deep breath as I concentrated on the road. Eve was behind me in her car, and I allowed the streetlights flashing above me to guide me to my destination. The older home with flowers and a manicured lawn was a welcome sight as I pulled up to the curb. I glanced at the porch light, but the living room was dark. Mrs. Harriet was visiting her children that night. I would miss her and her famous mint chocolate chip cookies. Sugary snacks were keeping me alive these days, it seemed.

Eve rapped on my door, and I exited my vehicle. I still had my saber strapped to my back, but my crossbow was in the trunk, and I lacked the energy to retrieve it. That was a tomorrow problem.

"Hey. Let's get you inside," Eve said.

I pulled myself from my vehicle and allowed Eve to lead me to my bachelor pad door. She held out her hand when we reached it. I immediately handed her my keys with the Kubotan attached. She unlocked my door and pushed it open before signaling me to enter.

Eve followed me inside before I slipped my leather jacket off and put it on the hook beside the door. "I will be okay. I just need some rest."

"Where are the potions I gave you? And your crossbow?" she asked.

"I have one of each potion in my jacket pocket. There are a couple more healing in the bathroom. My crossbow is in the trunk of my car."

Eve went to the small bathroom and opened the medicine cabinet. She grabbed one of the healing potions and returned with it. "Take this and go to bed. The quickest way for you to heal is with rest. It's a boon of both your human and demon physiology. I will go grab your weapons and bring them in. I know you have a small arsenal in that trunk."

I unstopped the cork and downed the potion. "But not my shifter?"

Eve smirked. "I'm no expert, but shifters don't seem to need as much sleep as humans."

Having a friend make you smile under these circumstances seemed like an unbelievable feat, but I chuckled. "I like you with the alpha. It is good for you."

"He's good to me, and that's what I would want for myself and any of my friends." She ducked outside and returned with my go bag full of weapons, including my crossbow.

"Thanks," I said.

She glanced around my small messy bachelor pad. We always went to Eve's house as Nishi was selling hers and mine was barely large enough for me, let alone three ladies. "Are you sure you don't want me to stay? My offer still stands. You could come back to my house."

I was well aware of who would be waiting for Eve at her house. I genuinely liked Hunter, but when he was done getting the hospital back to normal, he would be returning to Eve's house. Since sleep was the only thing on my itinerary for the next eight hours, there was no point in me ruining their evening more than I had. "I'll be fine. I live with the mundane and nobody knows where I am. After I crash for several hours, I'll be good as new."

Eve gave me a quick hug, then exited the apartment and closed the door. I sat at my small table to take off my boots and noticed the plate of cookies covered in saran wrap. While I wasn't surprised the landlord had cooked for me before she left, her kindness made my shoulders sag. I'd always been a one-man show and now I was surrounded by friends and the family from my past.

I was never one to pass on Mrs. Harriet's cookies, and I ate one in two bites before getting up and grabbing the milk from the fridge. Two cookies and a half glass later, I was crawling onto my bed fully clothed. Food took priority at a time like this, so I would undress and shower when I got up. The healing potion moved through me like a mother covering her child with a blanket. It was soothing, and I closed my eyes to enjoy the comfort of sleep.

The sound of breaking branches and howling roused me from my dreams of Greyson and the inventive things I could do with him in bed. Was I the only woman who was far more flexible in her dreams? Some of those moves weren't actually possible. Or were they? My waking brain wanted to return to the exciting images of my sexy warlock, but the insistent banging wouldn't allow the pleasurable escape.

The incessant thuds and sound of splintering wood made me realize that my dreams had turned into a nightmare. I glanced at the door as it shook from its frame, then rolled out of bed before having to grab the nearby table for support when I stumbled.

A few hours' rest was better than nothing, but I was hardly at a hundred percent. As I fumbled for my crossbow, I grabbed the bushel for my arrows and tossed it on the bed before grabbing the go bag and backing away from the door. It thumped when it fell at my feet and I grabbed an arrow, then loaded my bow as the door began to crack at its center.

My saber was still secured to my chest, and I realized I had slept with it on. That was a first and alerted me to just how out of it I was. Now I was thankful to have the weapon secured between my shoulder blades with my crossbow aimed at the front door. The howling and groaning had increased. Part of me wasn't sure if I was fully awake or if I was having a flashback from my youth when I had watched a Stephen King movie in my early teens.

The house shook with the force of whatever was behind my door, alerting me to the reality of my situation. This wasn't a nightmare; it was real, and more than one person was coming for me. Dagna had warned me there was a bounty on my head, but I hadn't taken it seriously. Of course, I was holding a bomb at the time and my priorities were averting the decimation of an entire city block. The groans continued until my door splintered and burst inward.

The horde that piled through my front door was similar to the victims I had met in the cemetery of Canton, Ohio. My bifron friend had gone to the trouble of finding fresher corpses, which had the capability to howl and groan, though none of the sounds were remotely human. These sick representations of their former selves lumbered toward me with their arms in the air as if they wished to embrace me.

I had watched enough zombie movies in the past to know how that would turn out. I didn't know if the zombies actually ate brains or they just killed you so they could lay more eggs in your dead body, but either way, those things were going down.

Most people would complain about such a small apartment, but the confined space stopped the horde from entering more than two at a time. With the kitchenette and sleeping area all in one room, they couldn't pilot in more than six bodies before my arrows started flying.

I hit the first two in the head and they fell onto my small

kitchen table, crushing it easily beneath their weight. The table legs snapped like dried firewood and skittered along the floor before bouncing into the fridge door. While I had picked up more arrows from Odin, I could tell by the bodies filing through my door that I didn't have enough for the seemingly endless horde outside. There was no way I was getting out of this alive without help.

My crossbow made a large thunk as it connected with an elderly gentleman in a high-end black suit. He had a white shirt and the pink carnation tucked into his suit pocket was fresh. Either the bifron had raided a mortuary or had gotten a hold of a body recently placed in a crypt.

I dropped a woman in a yellow chiffon dress next to him before I realized that none of my assailants had dirt on them. I grabbed two more arrows from the bushel on the bed, but I only had a few left. The gold bracelet Grayson had given me flashed against my wrist as I raised my crossbow again. He had told me to rub the runes he had inscribed on its beautiful surface. The problem was that I wasn't sure how it worked or how long it took to send him the signal. I quickly rubbed the strange symbols on my bracelet before returning to my quarry.

Four more zombies lumbered through the door, and I dropped an elderly woman in a floral dress and a man who looked like he was a lumberjack. He had blood on his flannel plaid shirt and a gash on his neck. Where the hell was the bifron getting these bodies? Was he killing people to implant his eggs?

The last of my arrows dropped the three zombies closest to me, and I tossed my crossbow on the bed and drew my Saber. This was why it had become my favorite weapon. You could run out of bullets. You could run out of arrows. But that sharp knife had never let me down, and I prayed it wouldn't now.

I quickly grabbed the throwing stars from the go bag and a small knife, then backed away to the corner of the room to give myself as much space as possible. The apartment still forced the zombies to funnel toward me, but there had to be at least a dozen between me and my door. How ironic I had phoned my son earlier to tell him I loved him, thinking that today was my last day. This wasn't how I expected to die.

My saber slashed in an arc and bit into the neck of my closest assailant. It bit in deep, almost severing the head from the clavicle and hung unnaturally to one side. Due to my lack of strength, it wasn't enough to remove the egg from its host and the zombie stumbled back before black filaments shot from the wound and repositioned the head into the correct position.

I switched tactics and flung one of my silver throwing stars directly at the zombie's forehead. It embedded deep, and the creature swayed back and forth before dropping to the ground. Learning that puncturing the egg within the skull was key, I released the rest of my throwing stars in succession. I had no intention of throwing my small knife. Once I ran out of the room, it would be my last resort when fighting in close quarters.

My saber arced again when a zombie with a plain white dress lumbered toward me. The blond woman looked to be in her late thirties and her petite neck split beneath my blade before her head fell to the floor. Her body followed seconds later as if it needed time to accept it was missing a vital component.

As my arms became fatigued, I turned so I could thrust backward with my saber, but with my strength waning I wasn't able to move out of the way of the other assailant climbing over the dead bodies piling into my apartment. Human fingernails slashed at my face and left thick grooves in my flesh as I tried to repel them.

The trickle of warm blood that dripped to the side of my mouth followed the burning sensation. The taste of copper may be an aphrodisiac for vampires, but the taste of my life force dripping to my lips made me nauseous. My movements were becoming increasingly clumsy, and the loss of blood would increase the effects.

I grabbed the small knife as more bodies clustered around me and a sea of arms surrounded me with pain and angry growls. My hand flashed with the small steel held within it as I stabbed everything I could get to. I may die, but I was taking as many of these bastards with me as I could.

There were so many things I wished I could say to my son. To Greyson and the friends I had made in Ravenholde. How ironic was it to gain the life you thought you never wanted, only to be sorry you never got the chance to appreciate it? At that moment, before my death, my thoughts went to Carnell. All the things I wished I had asked him. The truths about him and my father I never got to uncover. It was funny how you always believed you had more time. As the bodies crushed me against the wall of my own suite, I understood the value of love and sacrifice.

I had assumed the horde meant to rip me apart, but as they pressed me against the wall, I understood the true danger of the throng of bodies. My lungs burned as the breath was squeezed from them. Spots formed behind my eyelids as the groaning in my ears increased and the knife fell from my hand.

CHAPTER 14

My arms flailed in every direction before I clutched the sheets. I glanced around the room to find I was lying inside my covers. The banging at the door was real, and I heard my landlord yell.

"Faith, get up. I need you to report this."

"Coming!" I yelled, flipping back my covers.

I could understand a nightmare after the horrific events at the hospital, but I knew damn well I hadn't put myself into pajamas. Hell, I had never worn this pink sleep shirt in my life. It was surprisingly comfy and soft. My husband had thought it was hilarious to give me a Hello Kitty nightshirt and my son had laughed when I had pulled it from the gift bag. That had been my last Christmas with Luke, and I had kept the shirt because of the fond memory it invoked. But who had put me in it?

Eve had helped me home and had brought my weapons in. They were sitting on the table beside my go bag. The bushel was there also, but it was empty. I had gotten some from Odin. Where were they? With the nightmare still fresh in my mind, I searched the room for any signs of a struggle. Everything appeared exactly as it had when I arrived home last night.

The table was perfect, as was the door. I touch my face only to find the skin unmarred and smooth. My body was rested. I couldn't reconcile the events that I figured I imagined and my missing weapons. What the hell had happened last night?

"Faith!" Mrs. Harriet yelled.

"Sorry. I'm getting dressed." I pulled off the pink sleep shirt and dashed to my drawer before grabbing fresh undergarments and a Metallica T-shirt. That would combat the residue of pink left on my body from the shirt. My pants were all virtually the same with variations of black, blue, or gray. I chose my gray khakis and slipped my keys into my pocket before rushing to the door. I swung it open as Mrs. Harriet was about to rap once more.

My elderly landlord never looked mad or vexed, but the crinkles around her mouth alerted me to both. "I am sorry to wake you, but this is a disaster. Why anyone would prank an old woman like this is unconscionable."

I cleared my throat, trying to understand what she was saying. "You were visiting your kids, right? Did someone play a prank on you?"

"I'd say. I just returned home to find that monstrosity on my roof. It's going to bring the entire roof down. Not to mention the people flocking to the yard to take pictures. It's one thing to keep a statue on a downtown building, but my home is not built for this."

Had the demons done something to her? Were there remnants of the attack outside? "I don't understand. Can you show me what you are talking about?"

Mrs. Harriet was wearing a lilac-colored blouse and black dress pants. Like most people from her generation, she was particular about her appearance when traveling. Her flight must have got in an hour or two ago. She had only left for the weekend, and I had been in Canton for one of the days. "Come outside. And take a look." She left my door and walked toward the front yard while I grabbed my boots and quickly pulled them on.

The sun was shining and I could see people standing on the sidewalk in front of the yard, pointing at the house. My gaze moved to the flowers beside the stairs, to the porch, and onto the veranda. There was nothing out of the ordinary, yet two teenagers pulled out their cell phones and began taking pictures.

As they laughed and checked their phones to double-check the quality of the picture, I realized they had aimed at the roof. I jogged to the middle of the yard before turning and looking up.

The gargoyle was growling with its large canines exposed beneath the curl of its lips. Even in all gray tones, the eyes seemed to come alive and warn anyone away. Not a single person had stepped closer to take the pictures they wanted. The only blades of grass out of place were the ones beneath mine and Mrs. Harriet's feet.

Despite the anger the bulging eyes and extended teeth emitted, his wings were far scarier. They were completely upright and extended. The thick bones that made up the framework of those leather-like appendages when they were flesh and blood blocked out the sun and created a bat-like shadow on the base of the lawn. Every memory of Cal was a pleasant one. I couldn't remember a time when he had been harsh or unkind. This was the first time I had seen him in an attack pose.

To the mundanes this was a prank. A stone statue placed on an elderly woman's house to garner attention or a boost in social media follows. The supernatural community would know exactly what it was. Cal had declared war.

That wouldn't seem like much to most people, but then they didn't understand my uncle's true power. He could find almost anything in the human world, provided it had been here long enough to leave a trail. Artifacts. Books. Weapons. The rarer the better. His only weakness was his species' aversion to the sun. Similar to a vampire, he was tied to the lunar cycle. It wasn't the rays or brightness that made him turn his flesh to stone. It was an elemental part of his being. An innate aversion to being conscious during the day.

"Oh, no," I whispered.

Mrs. Harriet folded her arms, and her perfectly coiffed gray hair bounced as she wiggled her head. "This gargoyle and its companions typically reside on top of the Moreau building. Carnell has many versions of this statue and moves them around on a daily basis. I am not sure what kind of crane system he has up there, but you can only ever see the one from the ground. Somebody stole his statue and placed it on my roof. Didn't you hear anything last night? It must've made quite a ruckus."

I adored my landlady, but she was a mundane. The eccentric behavior of my grandfather was well-known in town, and I'd heard the story of his multiple gargoyle statues many times before. Since the sculpture altered positions on a daily basis, it was natural for the humans to assume he had several of them. The truth was so much simpler and scarier.

While the appearance of my gargoyle uncle on my roof was alarming, it also meant that my attack last night was very real. That didn't answer how I survived or how everything was magically put back in place. I held up my bracelet and turned it over on my wrist so I could inspect the runes etched on the surface.

I recalled touching the bracelet, attempting to reach out to Greyson. But I didn't remember him coming to my aid, or anyone else for that matter. Still, magic had been used to fix everything in my apartment, so either Eve or Greyson had saved me. Neither would know that the pink sleep shirt was a prank gift and I hope whoever it was got a kick out of putting me in it. Talk about adding insult to injury.

"Mrs. Harriet. I will take care of this. I promise the gargoyle will be off your roof after sundown."

"How are you going to do that? Do you have a contact with a crane company? I'm not sure how much it will cost, but…"

"My grandfather is Carnell Moreau. This is his statue, and I will have him retrieve it. There will be no cost to you, I promise."

Mrs. Harriet put her hand to her chest. "Carnell is your grandfather? He can't be old enough for that. He is so handsome." Just when I thought the pink shirt would be the most embarrassing part of my day. I should have known better.

"Yeah, he is older than he looks." Sure, that was true, but we looked about the same age. I had to start calling him uncle or some shit in the mundane world or just say he was a relation. Shit. I should know better. "Excuse me for a second. I left my phone in my suite." I jogged back toward my doorstep before more flashes went off.

I grabbed my cell phone from my jacket and hit Carnell's contact. He picked up on the second ring, though he had obviously been sleeping.

"Hello Faith."

"I need you. Cal blew a gasket and is currently perched on Mrs. Harriet's roof. He is in full combat mode, for Christ's sake. He is going to give her a heart attack."

"I am aware of his location," Carnell said with little remorse.

"Are you kidding me right now? Cal is going to be featured on thousands of social media posts in the next twenty-four hours. If he's lucky, he'll avoid being in better homes and gardens. This is a mundane community. What the fuck was he thinking?"

Carnell's voice dripped, and I detected the note of anger, but it wasn't aimed at me. "He was furious when Greyson called and alerted us to your current predicament. If your warlock lover hadn't given you the alert charm, you would be dead, and we would be in the middle of a zombie apocalypse. Cal will not be leaving your current residence until you find the bifron and end him. That egg-slinging demon has focused on you and won't stop until he kills you and plants one of his hatchlings inside you."

"I didn't realize bifron were so revenge oriented. I guess I should have."

"They aren't. They believe a worthy foe will produce a higher quality of offspring."

"The bifron wants me to be his baby momma. I think I just threw up in my mouth." I swallowed the bile and cleared my throat.

Carnell huffed. "Survival of the fittest sweetheart and you are the fillet mignon the bifron wants, thanks to the dozens of hatchlings you killed."

"I was surrounded. What happened to the dozen or so I didn't kill?"

"Your warlock used hellfire on them. It is quite effective on the hatchlings, but the bifron itself is far more sturdy. It would take minutes in such a fire with an open chest to kill that demon, and it is too intelligent to stick around for such an occurrence."

My gaze moved around my perfect apartment. "There's not a scorch mark in here."

"Greyson was exhausted after killing off your attackers. Eve relieved him and cleaned your mess in the magical sense. She put you to bed and ensured the entrance was warded, before she returned home. Cal made sure you had no further visitors until morning."

"I don't remember anything after the hatchlings tried to squash me."

"The more hatchlings the bifron creates, the more powerful he and the horde become. It has been purged for now, but it will grow again in record time," Carnell said.

"Understood. Finding that upchucking demon is my first priority. How do I get Cal back to the Moreau building? He can't move here."

Carnell was silent for a moment. "The answer is simple and one I have offered before. It will be much safer for you and your landlord if you move to the Moreau building. Your suite is already furnished and waiting for you."

I had been on my own for a long time and understood better

than most how imperative independence was. When Eve had refused to take Carnell's money and insisted on paying him back, I had understood better than anyone how important that was. "I don't want to live with you."

"I am not suggesting you live in the penthouse. You know there are several suites available, and I have one I think you would like. You don't have to answer right away, but I need to talk to you. Can you pop over so we can discuss our next steps?"

There really wasn't anything I could say. The only way to get my gargoyle uncle off my roof was to return the bifron to the Underworld, and I needed my grandfather's help. "Okay. I am on my way." I hung up the phone and grabbed my jacket.

I locked the suite on my way out, and had planned to call Greyson and Eve to thank them for saving me. Hell, my boyfriend had incinerated a zombie horde with hellfire while I had slept through it. I could just imagine that conversation starter. Oh hey, I heard you made some shake-n-bake demon while I was grabbing a nap. Are there curly fries with that? Did you save me any?

Oh yeah, that sarcasm was going to go a long way in the sorry about the apocalypse speech.

My landlady turned as I approached her on the lawn. The shadow from the gargoyle had spread as the sun moved to his back, and I smiled wanly at her. "It's all taken care of. Carnell will have the statue moved tonight."

She grabbed my shoulder and squeezed. "Thank you. I honestly don't know what I would do without you anymore. There will be a fresh batch of cookies waiting for you when you get home."

My phone chimed as I headed toward the Mercedes. I read the text and my heartbeat spiked as I read the two words from Odin. It's here.

I threaded my way through the cluster of people, but avoided anyone who looked like they wanted to chat about the statue on the roof. I jogged to the driver's door and jumped into the front seat before starting the engine. My tires screeched a bit as I pulled into the street and headed toward the Bloody Bucket.

While I was normally careful not to speed in town, my excitement got the best of me, and I threaded my way through the traffic. I wanted to get to the store before it officially opened, but as I considered the early time I realized that Odin was making an exception. His surplus store wouldn't open for another hour and a half and that confirmed he was just as eager for me to take down the bifron as I was.

He was hoping I would find that backstabbing witch Dagna in the process, and after that fiasco at the hospital, I was just as bloodthirsty as he was. My tire hit a small pothole in the Bloody Bucket parking lot as I pulled into the stall closest to the door. It jolted me from the fact I hadn't had my morning coffee, and I planned to rectify that on my way to the Moreau building.

I slammed my door in haste to exit my vehicle and was entering the Bloody Bucket to the chime of a dying weasel in seconds.

Odin was standing behind the counter. His wrinkled shirt and messy hair gave the impression he had slept in his truck, but I doubted that was the case. "Faith," he said as I entered.

There was no mirth and no flirting. This was a side of Odin I hadn't seen before. "Hey. Thanks for getting me this so quickly. I didn't expect you to open early."

"The bifron is spreading its curse and half the town knows about the attack last night. If Cal goes gargoyle berserker, a lot of people are going to die."

"I guess you heard about his taking up residence on my roof. My uncle is just… protective of me. He wouldn't hurt anyone."

Odin eyed me as if he were unsure if I was telling the truth. "You may want to read up on the reason the gargoyles were so feared in the Underworld and what led to their near extinction."

"It has to do with the dragons."

"Yes." He didn't seem to want to elaborate, and my gaze fell on the beautiful metal barrel of the flamethrower. The large weapon sat like a silver masterpiece on his counter, and my fingers slipped into the thick trigger before I could stop them.

I smiled as I lifted the heavy weapon. "Hello beautiful."

CHAPTER 15

I pulled into the alley behind the Moreau building. Carnell was standing at the top of the steps in front of the closed door. His arms were crossed, and he tapped his foot, alerting me to his impatience.

In all fairness, he wanted me to pick up the flamethrower. It was an essential part of my upcoming hunt for the bifron, and I had spent a little extra time with Odin.

The mechanics of the destructive weapon were simple, and it was ready to barbecue my demon foe. Odin's comments about gargoyles and his obvious wariness of Cal had made me wonder if there were things I needed to know about my stone uncle.

Those answers would have to wait. I did ask a few more questions. However, my dark magic dealer was unwilling to answer them. I doubted he would have said anything in the first place if he realized I had no knowledge of gargoyle history. Some extra investigation was warranted. For now, I had to be happy with my newest toy.

"What took you so long?" Carnell asked as I exited the Mercedes.

I tapped the trunk before ascending the stairs. "I just picked up a flamethrower from Odin. He was giving me a rundown on its operation. It's been a minute since I've used one."

Carnell opened the door. "I'm not sure what is more terrifying. The fact that you're excited about the prospect of using the weapon or that this isn't the first time you've used one."

I entered the building and glanced at the door that led to the gate in its basement. "How is Sharun doing?" I kept meaning to visit my demon cousin, but life kept getting in the way.

Carnell strode down the hall like he owned the place because, well, he did. He was quiet for a moment before he answered. "He performs his duties well, but he misses his family. It is a difficult transition."

The thought of missing anything about the Underworld was ludicrous to me, but then I had never been there. I had only heard bad things about the place. Many demons wanted to stay in the Underworld and remain protected from those that would create an imbalance. There were many members of the Underworld that I had come to love and respect. And I was beginning to accept that nothing was black and white. "I will visit him once we get this situation handled."

"He would like that." The elevator door opened before we neared it, and we entered before Carnell tapped the button for the sixth floor. It was the floor Cal lived on. I knew exactly where my brooding uncle was, and it wasn't in his suite.

"Why are we going to Cal's floor?" I asked.

The lift jolted upward. "I would like to show you the suite across from his. It would be far more convenient if you allowed your uncle to protect you here. Keep in mind, I cannot control his actions. Nobody, not even me, can order a gargoyle to do anything."

The elevator chimed before we exited the sixth floor. "Cal might be older, but he still listens to you."

"It has nothing to do with his age. Gargoyles were once royalty and since they are extremely hard to kill, it took the destruction of the dragon species to instigate their decline in numbers."

I paused in the hallway as we exited the elevator. "You make it sound like gargoyles are harder to kill than dragons."

Carnell walked to the door opposite Cal's. "They are. Gargoyles are not ruled by the sun in the Underworld. They can turn to stone at will and that includes parts of their body. They are practically indestructible."

"Then why are they dying off?"

"They have very few females left, and all are mated. There was an ancient scroll that said a lost demon bloodline that was banished to Earth centuries before the decline of the gargoyles had the ability to mate with them. Cal has searched for more years than you can count, yet has found no trace of it."

Yeah, there was definitely a lot more to my uncle than I thought, but his sordid history would have to wait. Still, as we stopped in front of the door, I glanced between the one Carnell had for me and my uncle's. "I will look, but I'm not agreeing to anything."

Carnell opened the door. "Of course."

My boots squeaked on the marble entrance of the spacious entryway. It wasn't as large as Carnell's, as he had an entire floor. However, there were only two suites on the sixth floor, which made the place massive for one person. The flecked tile opened into a large living area with tan leather coaches. I half expected to see faux fur and leopard print. It appeared my grandfather had taken my tastes into consideration.

The coffee tables were sleek, cherry wood with glass insets. A slate wall accented the white mantel and massive big-screen TV mounted above it. Two chairs matched the sofa with small side tables. The overhead lighting was subtle, but illuminated the entire room.

The floor plan was open, with a massive island in front of the kitchen and an oak table and chairs with a fruit bowl at its center.

Carnell had gone through a lot of trouble to decorate this place in muted colors. Even the pictures were of landscapes, which he knew I preferred.

Carnell moved his arm around the room. "There are two bedrooms. The main one has an en suite bathroom. You could set up the second for visitors." That was his subtle way of telling me to have my son for a visit. He wanted to meet him. Officially, that is. I had denied him that connection all this time. How did I bring my son to the supernatural world without revealing it?

"It's really nice." I had no intention of revealing my true hang-ups. They would only hurt Carnell, and I planned to deal with them. I just needed more time. "Let me think about it. I do like the fact that it's across from Cal. Let's talk about it again after I have dispatched the bifron."

"Fair enough," Carnell said and headed back toward the door. I followed without another word.

We re-entered the elevator and silently went upstairs to his penthouse. I followed him to his library and past the wall of orgies. I kept my eyes away from the floor where I had my last tryst with Greyson. Talk about returning to the scene of the crime.

I sat down on the chair in front of Carnell's desk as he took his seat. "I need a lead on the bifron. Where will this thing hang out? What is its next move?"

Carnell opened the file on his desk. "I put together everything I could on the species. Most don't even have human names. At least not ones we could pronounce. Have you talked to Kormack yet?"

"No. I was too busy being zombie bait, but I'm headed there next. I was hoping you could give me some direction first. I'm beginning to feel like I'm hunting blind on this one and the bifron has all the advantages."

He flipped through a few pages in the file. "You aren't wrong.

We have so little information on bifron. They are akin to a disease in the Underworld and feared even more."

I huffed. "I can see why."

"Speaking of zombies. Greyson noticed that some of the cadavers in your apartment had not been buried. We are watching the cemeteries, but we fear he is getting bodies from another source."

My fingers slipped into the pocket of my jacket and into the familiar grip of my kubotan. "I noticed that myself. What does the bifron eat? I know he implants the eggs in corpses and they consume it, but what is his food source?"

"Dead flesh. He consumes corpses that are too… expired for his children."

I grunted. "Should have seen that coming."

The comments that Carnell had made about me being a preferred host for the bifron's children popped into my mind. "You said this demon likes stronger corpses. He wanted me. The bifron may prefer a supernatural victim. The cemeteries aren't the only place where there are dead people. I think I should swing by the hospital morgue and then the supernatural one. Though ours has a protection spell, so the demon may avoid it."

"Go see Kormack first. He may have some information we don't."

I stood up. "Will do." I paused before exiting his private library. "Thank you for the suite. I will seriously consider it."

Carnell nodded, and I left, flipping my keys in my hand. The elevator was waiting for me, and I pressed the button to the main floor before it closed. Drin was there when it opened. I winked at him as he led me to the alley where my Mercedes was parked. Always the gentleman, he scooted down the stairs and opened my door before I got in. If I had more time, I would have played some show and tell with the monster weapon in my trunk, but I had three stops to make, and time wasn't on my side.

The jaunt over to Club Essence was quick. I assumed since

the sun was out that I wouldn't have to deal with the head vampire. The supernatural clubs never really closed, but there were few customers at this time of day. And the parking lot was practically empty when I pulled up.

I jogged to the front door and entered to find the lights on and less than twenty people sitting in booths. As I approached Kormack, my stomach flipped when I realized who my favorite empusa was speaking with.

Rhain turned to me and smiled. There was a droopiness in his eyes and while sunlight couldn't hurt him in here, he did look tired. "Faith, how can I be of service?"

I motioned to Kormack. "I want to ask him a few questions about our newest demon visitor."

Rhain smoothed his black tie with his hand. The gold ring on his finger was gaudy and ornate. "Another demon has used a token? Carnell has to get control of that gate, or he will be replaced."

I pointed at him, and my tone dripped with venom. "You want the job?"

Rhain shuddered. "Hardly. Nobody in their right mind wants that responsibility."

He wasn't wrong. The more I learned about my grandfather's duties to the Underworld, the more I didn't envy him. Nobody wanted that job, and it tied him to that gate and the Moreau building like a noose. Maybe that was why he created the club. He brought the fun to him. "You look tired Rhain. Long night?"

Rhain shrugged, and his immaculate silver suit moved like silk. "I'm a vampire, Faith. I can use an umbrella in sunlight to block the rays and it won't incinerate me, but the sun makes us lethargic. We can be up, but it's like a human being up for over twenty-four hours."

I had seen Rhain's blacked-out SUV at the council before. He had to travel during the day often for his duties there, but it hadn't slowed him down. Underground parking had its perks, I guess.

Rhain placed his palms on the table and pushed himself up. "On that note, I'm heading to bed. Enjoy yourselves." He sauntered away.

I sat down and smiled at Kormack. He was just as good-looking as last time, and I genuinely enjoyed visiting him. "I apologize up-front. This is a business call, but I need as much information as you have on the bifron."

Kormack's smile died on his face, and he leaned toward me. "A bifron is here? As in topside?"

"Yeah. It is up-chucking eggs like it's bulimic. I need any information you have on its species. We are already checking cemeteries and I'm hitting the morgues next."

Kormack thrummed his fingers on the table. "Most people assume the cemetery is the bifron's first choice, but it prefers corpses that it can implant its eggs without having to dig. Some eggs are not up to the process and die before reaching the corpse's brain. Bifron are a feared species in the Underworld. I am surprised any King would allow one off their island."

"I doubt they know. Everyone I've talked to fears these things."

"As they should. If this is an emperor, we are in for the fight of our lives."

I blinked as my fingers fisted on the table. "What is an emperor?"

Kormack ran his hand over his white dress shirt. "The oldest of the species has some shifting ability and can mimic other demons. It's a useful skill to lure a body. They will kill anything to host their children. Human. Demon. Their need to procreate and kill are their only instincts."

"The fact that they reproduce asexually makes it pretty easy for them."

Kormack shuddered. "It is unnatural."

"I agree," I said.

Kormack stared at me for some time. "I hear you have a new lover?"

Oh, hello awkward conversations 101. "Yes."

Kormack smirked. "And who is the lucky gentleman?"

"Greyson." Yup, always the queen of one-word answers when put on the spot.

Kormack's eyebrows arched. "That scrumptious warlock?"

My lips pursed, but I had to agree with his description. "Yes."

"You are very lucky," he said.

"I know. He's really good to me."

Kormack patted my hand. "As he should be. But if that magical piece of goodness doesn't keep you satisfied, please consider me."

I was used to being hit on, but Kormack's offer seemed like more. There was a hint of worry in his voice, and I didn't think he was trying to steal me from Greyson. I wasn't even sure he was offering sex. It seemed like something else. "Thank you."

"Anyone you choose is lucky to have you, Faith. In a room full of jewels, yours is the rarest."

Every time I saw Kormack, he made me feel better about myself. I knew he couldn't tell me anything more about the bifron, but he had given me the shifting tip. I stood up, then leaned over and kissed his cheek.

"What is that for?" he asked.

"Just for being you." I walked away before I did anything else out of character. Was I going soft? I had hugged two men and kissed another in the last twenty-four hours. And that didn't include sex with Greyson. The evolution of Faith was a slippery slope. I had to be careful I didn't end up at the bottom of an avalanche.

I jogged to my car and got into the driver's seat before heading toward the hospital. Hopefully, it was devoid of dark witches and magical bombs.

CHAPTER 16

I drove back to the hospital and parked three stalls down from the brown station wagon like I had last time. It must've been an employee of the hospital. I climbed out of my vehicle and then stopped by the trunk. While Greyson had assured me that my shrouded bushel of arrows would effectively hide any weapons I put beside it, the flame thrower was much larger than anything else in my arsenal. It was also a lot heavier.

It was mounted on a strap that secured to its owner's body to offset the weight. But it wasn't the kind of weapon I wanted to wander around the hospital with, even if no one could see it. I secured my crossbow and the additional arrows I had picked up at Odin's. My saber was secure under my leather jacket, as usual. Now I was ready for a visit to the mundane hospital morgue.

I flipped my keys in my hand as I entered the hospital. I parked in the back and used the same entrance I had last time, but this time I smiled at the orderlies as I navigated the hall. The nurse was pushing a cart with small white cups containing various medicines. She stopped at one of the rooms and ducked in as I continued to the nursing station.

"Which way to the morgue?" I asked the young nurse working at a computer at the desk.

She pointed to the side hall. "Just down those stairs on the right."

I nodded and skirted around an older gentleman pushing an IV stand on wheels. His ashen skin and droopy eyes alerted me he had already been a customer of that med cart as he shuffled his way into an adjacent room. The metal doorway to the basement was heavy. For the first time since entering the building, I was glad I had chosen to leave the flamethrower in my trunk.

A single set of stairs down and I reached the next level to find the morgue directly in front of me. I had already explored the basement level full of electrical equipment and had no desire to go back. I focused on the plaque with the name Dr. Clemons that was secured to the door. I turned the knob and entered the large room.

The bright lights shone down on the three silver gurneys, but only one was occupied. A white sheet lay over the body that the pathologist was preparing. His blue gloved hands grabbed for a scalpel before he turned toward me.

"May I help you?" he asked. The name tag on his white overcoat was the same as the name on the door. There was something familiar about his voice. He had a mask and cap covering his face and hair, so I couldn't tell if I had met him before.

I smiled at him. "I certainly hope so. I've been investigating a rash of disappearances. Thefts, if you will."

I pointed to the row of silver doors. I knew each cubicle held a chilled body behind its door. "The personal items of every victim are cataloged and sealed if you wish to investigate. I don't know if any of our guests were involved in criminal activity."

"No. I'm investigating the theft of dead bodies. Detective Bracken asked me to speak with local morgues and funeral homes."

"We are not missing anyone currently. I was not aware of any thefts."

I cleared my throat as the smell of death seemed to coat my mouth like cough syrup. "How can you stand the smell?" I said, before censoring my thoughts.

"It's a morgue. Death is kind of a thing here."

Thanks, Captain Obvious. How did I explain extrasensory olfactory glands to a mundane? "Yeah, I get that. It's just stronger than I thought it would be."

A sound of thumping erupted from one of the coolers and my eyes widened as the pathologist shifted from a man into the bifron. It ripped the mask and cap from its head, but it still wore the coroner's clothes. "So good of you to visit, Faith. I was hoping to run into you soon."

Being pissed at myself for not bringing a flamethrower to the morgue wasn't going to help, so I pulled my crossbow and two arrows as the bifron backed away. He hissed as the cooler door flipped open and a nude man in his forties tumbled to the floor. Three more cooler doors began to shake as I focused on the dead awakening from their slumber.

The bifron ducked into a back office as I dropped the man that had exited the cooler first. I dashed over to the door the bifron had escaped into, but found it connected to the hallway.

Every instinct in me wanted to chase the demon. Unfortunately, the hatchlings were breaking through and would wreak havoc on the hospital if I didn't put them down. I turned around as two women and an older man fell from the coolers to the ground. They groaned as they stood. Their eyes were focused on the ceiling.

I dropped all three of them in rapid succession. Then I retrieved my arrows before checking each cooler. The one thing I had learned in my first meeting with the bifron was the eggs took hold of a body almost immediately. After a few minutes of silence, I was sure I was safe. Now to find my lab-coat-wearing friend. Kormack had said the bifron could take another demon form. He hadn't said it could mimic a human.

I exited the morgue, sorry for the mess I had left in there. According to Carnell's research, the eggs dissolved once dead. Still, I would be informing him about the bodies. He and the council could decide if a more thorough cleanup was needed.

My hand slammed down on the hood of my Mercedes as I approached the driver's door. Yeah, I was still pissed I had missed my chance to barbeque that dead-head demon. At least I knew where he was getting his bodies. Most of those coolers had been empty. I needed to take a minute to compose myself before I ran off half-cocked and decided to call Nishi. I needed to see how she was doing. Her recent loss put everything in perspective. I had my phone out before I sat down in the vehicle.

Nishi picked up on the first ring. "Hey, Faith." Her voice still held a sadness, but it wasn't that gut-wrenching sound that I'd heard in the moments after Nathan's death.

"Hey. I just wanted to check on you."

"I'm good. I had an offer on my house but it's less than I want, and I would have to move quickly. I'm just not up for it yet," she said.

"Don't make a decision yet. I know a shifter that is selling her house in town to return to pack lands. Can I give her your number? She hasn't listed it yet."

"That would be amazing. Please have her call me."

Trauma and pain were always hard to gauge. There was a reason people continually asked how you were holding up under it. "How are you and the other hunters coping?"

"One day at a time. Trinity is taking it the hardest. She idolized Nathan. What is going on with you? I detect irritation in your voice."

I straighten my rearview mirror. "That's an understatement." I explained about the bifron and my repeated attempt to apprehend him.

"Where are you headed next? Do you have any leads on this undead demon?" Nishi asked.

"I'm going to check the supernatural morgue, but I'm pretty sure I just lost my best lead. He had converted the morgue in the hospital into his personal nursery. I really need to get my new office set up. It would be the perfect place to go and regroup. Since my bifron is on the run, I may pop by and check out the latest construction before I hit the next morgue."

Nishi was quiet for a moment. "Do you mind if I meet you there? I could really use a distraction."

"Absolutely. It would be great. I'd love to get your input on the design."

"See you there in ten," she hung up without another word.

I started the engine and pulled out of the parking lot, feeling much better about my missed opportunity than before I had talked to Nishi. It's funny how friends could do that.

I hit a drive-thru needing a caffeine fix. The large coffee burned its way down my throat, and I sighed as it hit my system. That black-bean juice was the nectar of the gods for me, and I had been stupid to try to start my morning without it. Unwanted gargoyle guests could really mess with a girl's morning routine.

I parked in front of my building and was getting out of the car when Nishi pulled up behind me. The front door was open, and I could hear the echo of a buzz saw coming from inside. As we entered the front door, I found my favorite golden Buddha inside. The floors hadn't been altered as the crew was focused on the industrial kitchen.

Nishi pointed to my gold good luck charm. "Are you keeping that?"

I rubbed the Buddha's head. "Yeah, I like him."

Nishi chuckled. "I do too. It totally fits your personality."

The noise of a buzz saw stopped, and I pointed to the stairs. "They are pulling out some of the kitchen, but I still want one here. Just not as large as the current one. The second floor has an open floor plan, and I was thinking it would make a great training studio for you. Nothing's been added so we could renovate it however you like."

Nishi zipped her short leather jacket higher as if she were cold. "Show me."

I led her upstairs, where I had first met Dagna. The boxes and mini kitchen the dark witch had set up for herself were gone. It highlighted how massive the room actually was. Floodlights hung down and illuminated the wooden floor, but there was no furniture to speak of.

I spun in a circle with my arms out. "This is it."

Nishi looked around. "Wow. This place is much bigger than I thought it was. I could turn this into an amazing dojo."

I winked at her. "And the rent is cheap since Carnell owns the building."

"I am not sure I need the entire floor. Are you going to build a couple of offices in here?" she asked.

"The shifter PI, Aurora, said she may need a new office. I could build two and give her one. That way, you would have an office as well."

Nishi's eyes moved around the empty room. "Faith, I think you just got yourself a tenant. Please build the other office for Aurora, though. I will feel greedy if I take all this space."

"Done. But don't worry. I plan to encroach on your dojo for training."

"You will always be more than welcome. I need all the help I can get with the trainees. Especially now."

Nathan had helped Nishi a lot with training and left her free to help both Eve and me. "I will be happy to put your rookies through their paces."

Nishi stared at me, but her smile fell, and she looked like a broken doll. She stood perfectly upright, but there was nobody behind the wheel. I shook her gently until she finally responded. "Sorry."

"What was that?"

"I blank out when I'm getting a magical download. Artemis is careful to make sure I'm in a safe environment before she blinks me out. She's concerned about the bifron. Apparently, it has caused plagues in the past. She says she needs you to kill it soon or we risk losing, well, everything."

"Yeah, the apocalypse shit. I keep hearing that. Does she have any idea where it is?" I asked.

Nishi pinched the bridge of her nose as if she had a headache. It wasn't surprising with a god uploading information directly into your brain. We were talking about copious amounts of data. "She said its primary directive is to procreate."

"Yeah. I keep hearing that too. It reproduces asexually, so it's dropping eggs by the dozen. I guess we will have to forgo the rest of the tour so I can hunt that thing. Usually, I am stoked about taking down a demon, but this thing actually scares me."

"Because it wants you. It believes it will have stronger babies from supernatural hosts, and has fixated on you," Nishi said.

"Yup. But that means, despite the protection wards, it's going to try for the supernatural morgue."

Nishi nodded. "That is what Artemis thinks as well. Since I'm already out. I will follow you to the morgue. Let's see if your latest admirer has made a play for our dead people."

We jogged down the stairs, our thick boots thudding in the narrow corridor until we exited at the bottom. Dust rolled through the sunlight as it filtered in from the open front door. This place would be home soon, but I had an undead criminal to catch and one of my best friends at my side.

Nishi stopped me by my vehicle. "Do you know how to kill this thing? Artemis said you have to incinerate the heart, and it's very difficult to get at."

"Let me introduce you to Texas."

Nishi frowned. "The state?"

"Nope. That's what I named my new weapon." I opened the

trunk, and she flipped back the black blanket I had covering the flame thrower.

Her fingers traced the thick metal barrel. "Holy shit. Why did you name it Texas?"

"What is big and has the best BBQ?"

Nishi chuckled. "Texas."

CHAPTER 17

I drove behind the local Kroger and parked in the alley. The Grim Vale was neatly disguised in plain sight. The sancorous spell kept it hidden behind a thin mist only the supernatural community could see. Carnell owned this building and rented it to the council, so they retained control of the area. I wondered what the mundanes saw when they glanced back here. A row of garbage bins or pallets? Anything that wouldn't pique their interest.

The sancorous spell possessed an aversion component and they would avoid this area in the same way they did the prison. It was comforting to know I didn't have to watch out for the mundanes while I was investigating whether my bifron friend had infiltrated Grim Vale Morgue.

Nishi stopped as we passed through the mist that shrouded the building from the mundane world. "Maryam has three assistants. If this demon can shift into anyone, how do we determine if someone in the morgue has been copied?"

I paused and surveyed the building. It was the size of a small bungalow with a gray stone exterior and a large picture window in front with the name of the morgue painted in gold paint. "The bifron smells like he died a week ago. If you get a whiff of decay and rot, then call me. I will talk to Maryam while you interview her employees. There is no guarantee he's here, but he is bound to show up sooner or later. I thought the wards would deter him, but I don't think they work that way."

Nishi put her hand on her kris knife and froze for a moment. "You are right. The wards won't work on him. They simply shroud the location from mundanes and avert discovery. A demon is part of the supernatural world, so he can walk right in. I think Greyson will have to revamp the spell."

"Damn. I should have asked about that. I assumed protection spells meant that random demons trying to start an apocalypse wouldn't be allowed to enter."

"Yeah, that would make sense. But unfortunately, they need the bodies of any supernatural brought here. If they put a protection spell for demons, then Carnell would have to deal with them."

"Makes sense. Let's go." We entered the reception area where the woman behind the large oak desk was putting a file into the computer. I tapped my hand on the wood to get her attention.

"How may help you?" the receptionist asked.

"I need to speak with Maryam. And can you tell me how many people are currently in the building?"

"Just Maryam, Scott, and me. Maryam is in the morgue and Scott is prepping a body for transport," she said.

I had been to the morgue once before and knew where Maryam's morgue was located at the end of the hall. "Thanks. Nishi just has a few questions for you and Scott." I headed down the hallway to the sign that read morgue and passed the rooms where the bodies were prepared for the double doors at the end.

After the large metal doors swung back behind me, I noticed Maryam leaning over a body on a gurney. The sheet was partially pulled back to the woman's chest. Maryam was wearing blue scrubs and had a mask and cap similar to the one the bifron had worn in the human morgue. The main difference was that she didn't have on a lab coat. Instead, she wore a lamp on her head as she inspected a wound on the dead woman's temple.

The green walls were a different color than that of the mundane morgue, but the rows of small cooler doors and the undertone of decay were the same. I wrinkled my nose as I approached the studious pathologist. She remained focused on her current subject.

"Hey Maryam," I said.

She glanced up and began to pull off her blue rubber gloves. "Faith, it's good to see you. What brings you to this neck of the woods?"

"A bifron. It's grabbing bodies from the cemetery and the hospital. It is only a matter of time before it comes here looking to spread its infection. I came to warn you and secure the area."

Maryam tossed her used gloves on the metal roller cart by the body. "I have never studied a bifron. I'm required to familiarize myself with the physiology of any species that lives in or visits our realm. Why haven't I heard of it?"

"Bifron are banned. And for good reason. They are confined to a single island in the Underworld. Even the demons fear them. Think zombie apocalypse on steroids. They implant their eggs in dead corpses and control them until the egg matures into an adult."

"That is interesting and terrifying. I haven't seen anything like that here. But I appreciate you telling me about the eggs. If the bifron is controlling corpses, they must implant in the brain so they can control the nervous system of its host."

My fingers inadvertently slipped into my jacket pocket and into the security of my kubotan. "Yes. The egg enters its host's skull and controls it from there. I need you to put a temporary ward around the morgue to deter demons."

"That is impossible. We have bodies sent in from all over the world. Many representatives are demon. It may deter the dead as well."

"I was recently told that. However, a bifron infection is worse than having the demons inconvenienced for a couple of days while I track this thing down."

Maryam removed the headlamp and put it on the rolling cart. "What does this demon look like?"

"It has the ability to take human form. It looked like the human pathologist at the hospital when I saw him half an hour ago. I'm guessing he can impersonate anyone. Honestly, I don't know what his shifting criteria are."

"Damn. That is unnerving. Okay. I will put Grim Vale on lockdown until I hear from you. Greyson will have to enact the wards if you are looking for that kind of security."

"I will get him on it right away, but in the meantime, we need to check your dead and make sure they are clear of infection. Nishi is interviewing your staff as we speak." I sent a quick text to Greyson and was pleased to find out he could enact the wards remotely. Things were finally looking up, and I felt I had gotten a step ahead of the bifron for a change.

Maryam and I both glanced at the ceiling when we heard a static charge above us. "Greyson said he could put the extra protection spells up remotely."

Maryam nodded. "He has access to every security system. That's convenient. I have to send a message to the remote offices that we can't accept demon bodies for a couple of days. We don't get an overabundance of them, anyway. The perks of immortality and all."

The double doors swung open before Nishi walked through. Her dark eyes and long black hair accented her creamy skin. She was short like me, but slender. "The staff are clear. I heard the wards go up. Do you want to check the perimeter before we go? We should make sure there is nothing inside. I noticed a transport truck outside. Is it empty?"

Maryam shook her head. "Those bodies have been autopsied and are headed back to the families."

"How many bags are in the truck?"

"Four," she said.

I sighed. "Let's check it out."

I followed Nishi from the morgue and out the front door. She pointed to the walkway beside the building where the white transport truck was parked by a side door. "This must be connected to one of the prep rooms. I should have stopped in there on the way to the morgue."

We were walking toward the truck when I noticed a flash on the ground. It glinted from the motion sensor as we approached the door. No doubt because they delivered bodies at all times of the night. As soon as I knelt down, I recognized the coin. "Shit. The bifron expected there to be wards around the morgue. This is a nullifying coin. It is either here or on its way."

Nishi pulled her kris knife. "I doubt Dagna wanted to get near the bifron. She likely dropped it here so it could approach at its leisure. What do we do?"

I rushed to the side door and passed a body in the prep room. It was on a gurney with a sheet over it. A black bag was folded on the counter with jars and other implements I didn't recognize. I dashed back to the morgue and through the double doors.

Maryam was in the process of putting her headlamp back on. "That was fast."

"The bifron is either here or en route. The wards have been breached. We need to get the dead bodies out of here. Can they all fit in that transport truck?"

"No. It will only hold eight and I have ten total in the facility."

"Help us load what we can, and we will come back for the rest. We can start with the body in the room beside the truck."

Maryam dropped her light and covered the woman she was working on with the sheet, then followed me to the adjacent room. She grabbed the black bag, and we gently laid out the long cover before pushing the cadaver onto its side and placing him into the bag. We were rolling the gurney he was on outside when Nishi glanced at the transport truck.

"Ladies, I think we have a problem."

I jogged to the back so I could see inside the cargo truck. Two black bags had sat up. "We're too late. He already implanted the eggs." Again, I had left my flamethrower in the trunk of my car, but only because it was so close to the facility. "I will be right back."

Nishi took a fighting stance as I ran to my Mercedes and grabbed the flame thrower. Texas was a beast of a weapon, and I had no doubt my arms would feel like jelly after a few minutes of use. I affixed it to my shoulders and secured the strap before jogging back to the transport truck.

The hatchings had either unzipped their body bags or ripped their way out and were lumbering from the rear exit of the van. I had placed the ax my grandfather had given me under my jacket so my bifron friend wouldn't see it. The flame thrower would deter him but not kill him and I wanted him to think he had the advantage.

Nishi howled as she stabbed a man crawling toward her with her kris knife. I had already explained how to kill the hatchlings, so the man slid off her blade when it pierced his eardrum.

There were three more bodies exiting the truck when I aimed toward it. "Nishi back up. Let's see how fire-retardant those fuckers are."

Nishi backed toward me, and I waited until she was beside me and the zombies were a few feet away from the truck before I pressed the trigger of the flamethrower. I recognized the face of the human pathologist from the hospital and wondered how he had gotten to the supernatural morgue. Had the bifron brought him here? Did he have a magical heritage I was unaware of? Neither answer changed what was in his head. The flame exploded from the thick barrel of my flamethrower and made me step back a bit from the recoil.

The two men in front of Dr. Clemons were immediately engulfed in flame and their skin sizzled as they continued to try to reach us. They staggered and fell as their flesh was consumed and we coughed through the smell of burnt flesh in the air.

The human pathologist smiled, but his skin did not ignite like his human friends. He backed away from the fire and shifted to his natural form. "I will see you soon, Faith." He darted down the alleyway and disappeared around the corner.

Nishi turned to me with her kris knife drawn. "What do we do?"

I jiggled the large weapon in my hand. "I can't sprint with this thing. He will shift to a human form as soon as he is out of sight. We need to track him in the mundane world. Greyson needs to fix the wards and we need to double check there are no more hatchlings on site before we leave."

She nodded, but her eyes remained on the alley where the bifron fled. "Agreed."

"This bifron is really starting to piss me off." I swung the weapon to the side, so it rested on the thin strap over my shoulder. I took out my cell phone and clicked my contact. It rang twice before he picked up.

"What do you need, Faith?"

"Hi, Detective Bracken."

CHAPTER 18

"This is the deal. I'm tracking a serial killer and grave robber. This guy is one sick bastard, and he enlists the help of those around him." Yeah, I was embellishing like a teenager with a Bedazzler, but I needed information and Detective Bracken was my best source in the mundane world.

"A serial killer? Are you sure?" he asked.

"Yeah. This guy's bad news, and he has evaded Interpol on many occasions. You won't have him in your system, but you will start getting odd reports from graveyards, morgues, and funeral homes." Thank god my nose wasn't made out of wood because it would be about 3 feet long after that Interpol remark.

"Dammit. We have already gotten several reports of disturbed graves. Are you telling me he stole the bodies?"

"In some cases. In others, he just mutilates them. You will find bodies stabbed in the head, set on fire, and cut to shreds." It was easier to seed the mundane police with a grave-robbing mangler than try to explain a bifron. The monster was real. He just wasn't human. I also left out the part about me mangling those bodies, but describing the egg-sucking hatchlings was a no-go.

"I will have the cemetery confirm that the graves that were

disturbed are empty and we will get the entire department looking for this guy," Det. Bracken said.

"That's what Interpol did, and he fled. If we aren't careful, we will effectively send him to another innocent town. I have a lead to somebody that could either be an accomplice or a victim. Let me check it out and I will get back to you. Give me twenty-four hours before you call in the calvary and I promise to take this criminal down." That was at least the truth.

There was a shuffling of paper through the phone line and several clicks on a keyboard before the detective answered. "I will give you until tomorrow morning. I can't leave a sicko like this on the streets if you haven't apprehended him by then."

"Agreed."

"Faith, I do appreciate you coming to me. You seem to have some powerful contacts. What do you need?"

Yeah, I felt like a shmuck. He wasn't wrong, but those contacts were demonic or empowered. I almost laughed at the thought of Cal as an Interpol agent.

"I need some information. An address for the pathologist who works at the hospital. His credentials were used to remove some bodies. I am hoping to find him alive and unaware of the theft." That wouldn't happen, but I didn't want to sully the mundane's name. I would clear him of any charges later, but his identity was my best lead right now.

The clicking of keys echoed in my ear. "I know Dr. Clemons. He is a good man. I worked on multiple cases with him. He is a little forgetful, so I won't be surprised if he isn't aware his credentials were nabbed."

"I figured as much. Put out an APB on his credit cards and on him. This guy is a master at identity theft. Your people will think that it's Dr. Clemons, but it's really our killer."

"I hate the ones that impersonate their victims. You don't think Dr. Clemons is alive, do you?" Det. Bracken asked.

I should lie until my grace period was up, but I respected the detective too much. "I'm sorry. The chances of that are slim."

He cursed under his breath. "I appreciate your honesty. I am texting you Dr. Clemons' address and information. I have added the APB and will notify you if anything pops up." He hung up and my phone chimed.

My police scanner would alert me to those same APBs so I wouldn't be waiting for Det. Bracken's call. Not that I didn't trust him. The police would investigate any reports and wouldn't alert my detective friend until after one was confirmed. I needed to intercept any bifron sightings. The mundanes couldn't handle my demon convict and I didn't want anyone to get hurt.

Nishi's phone chimed as I hung up. "Hey Trinity, what is up?" She rubbed her forehead as she listened to the youngest of her hunters. "Settle down. You are getting worked up for nothing. What happened to Nathan isn't your fault. And Artemis doesn't make mistakes. I will be back in ten minutes." She hung up.

I touched her arm. "I am really sorry about Nathan. It must be hard for everyone. Det. Bracken gave me the address for the human pathologist. I doubt the bifron will go there but I plan to check it out. See to Trinity. She needs you more than I do."

Nishi nodded. "Thanks for the distraction." She strode away with the confidence of a hunter, but her eyes remained haunted. I wished there was more I could do for my friend, but time was the only thing that healed a wound like that and even then, it wasn't a permanent fix. Memories reared up when you least expected and there was no antidote for a lost love.

I walked to my car and popped my trunk before placing Texas under the black blanket. My conversation with Det. Bracken and Nishi had given the barrel of the flamethrower time to cool down, but it was still warm. The jeweled ax was still hooked inside my leather jacket, and I decided to leave it there. It was small enough not to hinder me while driving and I would be investigating the pathologist's home before bringing the flame thrower inside. Burning down a mundane house was not on my to-do list, but it was a real possibility.

My boot kicked gravel along the pavement in the back alley of Kroger. I was outside the shrouding mist that hid the Grim Vale morgue and it appeared dreary and uninviting when looking at the rusty garbage cans on either side of the laneway with light fog in between. I opened my door and sat down before starting the vehicle. The lane led to the main street, and I was inputting the address Det. Bracken had given me in my GPS as I drove. I was forced to use my phone since the Mercedes had that safety feature that wouldn't allow me to drive while adding an address. Vehicles were so uppity about safety. I wondered how they felt about a demon apocalypse.

Dr. Clemons lived on a street named Westerhill. I hadn't driven on it before, but followed the route my phone directed me to. The rolling lawn and manicured trees outside the white house with black trim denoted a man who took pride in it. The red rose bushes beside the porch were in full bloom and illuminated by the porch light. There was only one light on in the living room and it appeared to be a tall stand-up lamp.

There was no movement in the house and no other car in the driveway as I parked. Dr. Clemons had driven to work, but he had never returned. Still, the bifron had taken his identity, and I had to confirm there wasn't more to it than opportunity. Would the bifron maintain his fake host's identity to spread his disease or did he enjoy pretending to be someone else? It was more likely it gave him the opportunity to kill and plant his eggs, but he still had many dead resources available to him, and I assumed he would use those first.

Not because the bifron cared about anything except its young. But it took time to lure one individual, kill them, and implant them with an egg. It was far more time conscious to seed an entire cemetery or morgue. It would look for an easier and more time-conscious location.

I glanced at the double swing on the porch as I ascended the steps to the oak front door. It had a lion's head brass knocker, and I rapped the ring in the lion's nose against the brass plate. I had no idea if Dr. Clemons was married, and I didn't want his wife or girlfriend becoming the bifron's next victim. After not receiving an answer, I glanced down the street but found no cars, so I knelt down and pulled out my picklock set.

The tumbler clicked on my second attempt and while the home was beautiful, the security was almost nonexistent. In this high-end mundane area, neighbors looked out for one another, and I quickly closed the door as soon as I was inside.

The entrance area was large, with a thin pine table with several pictures and a bowl with potpourri on it. It gave off a faint smell of cinnamon and oranges, and I inhaled deeply as I walked into the living room. The lone lamp I had seen from the driveway was on, but nothing moved. The floral couches denoted a woman's touch with pink cushions that picked up the tones in the design. Like the table at the front entrance, there were several photos of Dr. Clemons and a blond woman with a kind smile.

I moved to the kitchen and found the white marble countertops were perfectly polished and the coffee pot was cold and half full. Most women would pour out the excess, but maybe Dr. Clemons' wife was away. God, I hoped so.

The dining table was large and round and had a lace doily in the middle with a bowl of fruit, but there were only two apples in it. I doubled back to the stairs close to the entrance and jogged upstairs. The main bedroom was on the right and as soon as I entered, I knew where Mrs. Clemons was.

The boxes were stacked in the corner of the room, and one side of the closet was empty. They were marked for donation, and I was about to assume they were getting a divorce until I saw the paper clipping beside the bed. I read Rita Clemons' obituary and placed it back on the side table when I was finished. I hoped they were reunited in death because life had not been that kind to them.

I double-checked the other rooms only to find them empty. The bifron had not come to Dr. Clemons' house, but then he may not have had the address. Being able to duplicate the man's body and read his memories were two different things. He had taken the doctor's clothes, which likely included his credit card. Would he stay in a public place? The questions continued to mount but the answers remained elusive. Damn.

I exited the large home quietly and returned to the Mercedes. The scanner was on and lying in the passenger seat as I contemplated my next move. Where would a demon go if he was wearing his favorite skin suit? I grabbed my phone and read the information Detective Bracken had sent me while I was investigating the house. Since they had pulled the doctor's credit card records, they had a list of restaurants frequented by the human pathologist. With nothing else to go on, I decided to scout the locations.

The Waverly turned out to be a pub frequented by police. I sat in the parking lot and stared at the men at the bar. They laughed and clinked their glasses together and though they were not in uniform, there were several with badges clipped to the pockets of their blazers. Dr. Clemons had worked with these men for years, so I could see him coming here for a beer after work. Especially after the loss of his wife.

The next location on the list turned out to be a diner with several booths. It was older and had been in business when I had lived here as a teen, but I had never eaten there. I hadn't fit in with any crowd really and had avoided public spaces with the rare exception. As soon as I had realized the Waverly was frequented by cops, I had left. The bifron wasn't stupid enough to try to fool them. A casual dining restaurant was another thing altogether. These people wouldn't know intimate details about

Dr. Clemons. I was about to exit my vehicle when static echoed from the scanner.

"I got a tip that Dr. Clemons has been sighted at the Dirty Dog. Please advise," an officer said.

I started my car and peeled out of the parking space. I knew exactly where that dive bar was, and it wasn't on the list of locations Detective Bracken had sent me. There was no way the real Dr. Clemons would visit that kind of establishment. My vehicle weaved through the few cars I found on the road as I sped toward the Dirty Dog.

The Dirty Dog was a mundane bar and not a good one. The problem wasn't the clientele, though. How would I get the demon outside? It would be busy, and the tables were too close together to use the flamethrower easily? Not to mention, I couldn't unleash Texas in a populated area. I was pretty sure Kentucky fried biker wasn't on the menu. If I threatened it, then the bifron may resume its natural form and that presented an even scarier scenario.

There was no way I could leave the bifron to the police. The department had just authorized the officers who called in the tip to take Dr. Clemons in for questioning. I had all of five minutes before they reached the Dirty Dog.

Since I hadn't waited for anyone's approval, I was already pulling into the parking lot and trying to decide which weapon I was going to use on the bifron. Laughter and music echoed from the front door as I approached. It was a good day for a demon to die. I just hoped it wasn't me.

CHAPTER 19

I entered the thick wooden door to the sound of laughter and clinking glasses. A long wooden bar looked the same as the last time I had visited. Few of the leather stools were empty, but those remaining few were ripped.

The slew of tables was occupied by large men in leather vests. Most had beards and logos on the lapels. A few men were playing darts, but they weren't any good and several more were clustered around a green pool table at the back.

My gaze moved over the patrons. Many grabbed the single menu cards from the table and though the food did not smell that appetizing, I was sure the kitchen was about to get a rush. These men were looking to fill the hole in their gut and almost anything would do. A waitress in a short black miniskirt approached me.

"You don't need to wait to be seated here, honey. Grab any open spot you like," she said as she placed a beer in front of a man in a plaid shirt at the table next to me.

"Sorry. I am meeting a friend. I am just seeing if he is here yet."

She flicked her hand toward the bar. "Feel free to wander. Just be careful of Maverick. He gets handsy when he is drunk." I had no idea who Maverick was, but an over-friendly biker was the least of my problems.

I blinked, but recovered from my shock as Dr. Clemons raised his hand to garner my attention. That demon bastard wanted me to find him. My flamethrower was in the car, but I had my ax under my jacket. I just couldn't kill him with it. I plastered a smile on my face as I threaded my way to the table near the rear of the bar. He had chosen a table closest to the washrooms and the rear exit. Smart.

"Hello, Dr. Clemons. What a surprise to find you here. This isn't your typical hang out." I took a seat opposite of him at the table.

The bifron pushed the full beer away from him. "You know I am not that pathetic doctor. My name is Reoul. I don't typically bother with names, but you have proved a worthy adversary. Your understanding of my species is limited, but you have anticipated my moves. I am almost sorry that will have to change. I have become quite fond of our game."

"Everyone keeps telling me that your only instinct is to procreate, but you aren't lying. You chose a location the doctor wouldn't have come. Do you know anything about your victims?"

"I consumed this vessel. It is the only way to recreate it. While I can't duplicate all his memories, baser instincts can be discerned. He would have chosen a family-type establishment. I chose this location for you."

"You have never been topside, yet you seem to have more than a basic understanding of human culture. Is that because of your children's hosts?" I asked.

"Of course not. I studied in the Underworld prior to my arrival. I needed to accomplish certain tasks to ensure my children's survival."

"The demon who sponsored your visit topside. He can't expect you to stick to any bargain you made with him. Surely he knows you will kill him and plant an egg in his skull the first chance you get."

Reoul leaned closer to me, and his eyes glowed with an unnatural red glint. "What makes you think the aspiring King of Hell is a man?"

I thrummed my fingers on the lacquered table, then wiped them on my pants when I hit something sticky. "Are you saying it is a woman?"

Reoul shrugged, and I couldn't decide if he was messing with me or stalling. Either way, I was running out of time and the police were on their way. "What do you want?"

"For my children to flourish on earth. Is that not the goal of any parent?" he said.

"Sure, but that isn't going to happen in your case. Your species needs to be confined to the Underworld for everyone's safety. They have a nice little island all sectioned off for you."

Reoul hissed. "There is nothing nice about it. We are forced to implant in the dead of our own. I never had more than five children, and several died due to poor living conditions. They deliver us animal carcasses. It is despicable."

"And you can't survive on dead animals?" I asked. I had no idea what kind of animals roamed the Underworld, but I felt sorry for them.

"Yes, but they taste terrible. I imagine it is like a human becoming a vegetarian. It is an awful existence," he said.

"Yeah, that is not awful. Your species is just going to have to deal with it. You, on the other hand, will not be around to see it. I was given a kill order for you."

Reoul's shoulders shook when he laughed. "Had you been able to kill me, you would have. You lack the weapons needed for such a feat. I am an emperor of my species. That comes with certain fringe benefits."

"Does this weapon have a jeweled handle by chance?" I taunted.

The bifron's eyes widened, and he glanced around the bar. "You will not attack me in such a busy location. By the next full moon, your species will be enslaved, and I will no longer need to use my human disguise."

I froze. "The next full moon? That is a very specific date. What happens then?"

Red and blue lights reflected off the walls and I knew I had less than a minute before the police came through the front door. The bifron's eyes darted to the exit, but my description of my ax handle spooked him. Would he make a run for it, or was he weighing his options?

The door burst open, and four police officers stood at the entrance. They put their hands on their gums and their stance gave the impression they were dead serious about using those weapons. "We just want Dr. Clemons. He is in the bar. Stand aside and let us apprehend him and you can go on with your evening."

The men in this bar did not typically cooperate with the police, but Dr. Clemons was not one of theirs and several men shrugged as if they couldn't care less. The officer took out his phone and glanced at the screen. He was likely looking at a photo of Dr. Clemons and I waited for my bifron to dart down the hallway beside us. I didn't expect him to hold up his hand.

"I am Dr. Clemons. How can I help you, officer?"

The four policemen approached the table slowly, and one leaned toward me. "Det. Bracken told us you might get here ahead of us. Please step aside. The force appreciates you helping with this investigation, but we can take it from here."

The young cop believed what he was saying. He felt he was protecting me and that he and his buddies were simply apprehending a suspect. Det. Bracken didn't think Dr. Clemons was involved in the killings. He thought the poor man's ID was stolen. They had no idea how much danger they were in once they got this demon alone. I wasn't sure the back of a police cruiser could protect them from a bifron. The thing had few weaknesses.

Reoul stood up and nodded politely. "I will do whatever you ask of me, sir." He held his hand out. "Do you need to cuff me?"

The officer nodded. "Just until we have this straightened out. We will get this all sorted out back at the precinct. I promise." He took his cuffs from their holder and snapped them onto the bifron's wrists. I had no idea what this demon was playing at, but there was no way I left it alone with the mundane police.

I stood up. "I need to talk to Det. Bracken about this guy. There is more going on than you realize. He is dangerous."

The other three police kept their hands on their weapons, and it was obvious they were taking my threat seriously. Had I been staring at the frail-looking pathologist, I am not sure I would. The young officer led Reoul through the scattered tables of men. The demon shuffled along with his head down, looking suitably miserable as he followed his captors. His act didn't fool me, but I had to go along until I could spring the demon and enact that kill order.

There was no doubt the bifron would try to kill me once I pulled that ax, but I needed my flamethrower. I had mentioned the ax on purpose, as it alone wouldn't kill Reoul.

The young cop held the door open to the bar as Reoul exited the place and stood just outside. He glanced at me before he smiled and pulled his cuffs apart as if they were made of aluminum foil. Everything happened at once.

The cops behind him shouted for me to get down and the claws sprung from Reoul's human fingers before he slashed the young cop across the chest. The cop grunted and grabbed at the torn fabric but as a mundane the poison was attacking him much quicker than it had me, and I launched toward him as Reoul bolted from the bar.

There wasn't a lot of time, so I grabbed one of the healing

potions and knelt by the cop's side. One of his buddies kneeled beside me. "What is that?"

"Antivenom. The doctor is using snake venom in those fake claws that spring from his shirt. This will counteract the poison. If he doesn't drink it now, he will be dead in two minutes." I poured the vial into the young cop's mouth as his partner held him down. He was already going into convulsions, but I wouldn't let a young man die because he didn't understand the world he had entered. He swallowed the potion and his body calmed.

The cop clicked his mic. "Officer down. Dr. Clemons is on the loose. He is armed and dangerous."

"That isn't Dr. Clemons. He is an impostor. The real Dr. Clemons is dead, but I doubt you will find his body."

"This is one sick perp," the dark-haired officer said.

"Your partner will live. I have to get this guy before he moves to another town." I didn't wait to see if he would try to stop me. The other two officers were attempting to keep the patrons in the bar, not wanting anyone near the fallen officer.

The area was remote, and I knew we were only a few blocks from the mall. I didn't think the bifron would prefer a mundane neighborhood, but none of its actions had made sense. It had enjoyed baiting me and that wasn't in the bifron handbook. There was more to these demons than just procreation. They liked a good taunting.

I stopped in a dark alley behind a closed restaurant. I could see the Moreau building in the distance and had a pretty good idea of what my demon friend wanted. I pulled out my phone and sent a text. My doppel big brothers had never let me down, and I knew they wouldn't now. It was time to go on the offensive. "Hey Reoul. Why not stop and chat for a bit? Surely you aren't scared of a small ax."

The sound of a cat hissing echoed around me, and I sprinted forward. No animal would be fooled by the demon's skin suit, and I caught sight of Reoul running on a side street before running after him. He took several back alleys before he made it to Raven Street.

I glanced at the sign above me and realized it was an underground parking garage. It was right beside the Moreau building, but it had access to the club. Many patrons parked here, and I had suspected the bifron may take this less traveled route. He stepped out from behind a parked car as I moved toward one I recognized. "Faith, this has been quite a treat. Unfortunately, I must cut our visit short. I promise to come back soon, and we can have a more intimate conversation."

I chuckled. "Did you honestly think you were going back to the Underworld to ride out this little storm? Carnell would never accept a token from you. The new Sharun can see through your petty disguise. There are several new security measures, and you will never leave this parking garage alive."

"You don't honestly believe you can kill me? Surely you have learned the folly of those attempts by now. I will use your body after I kill you to raise my young. I am sure you will make a suitable mother, but your stupidity is concerning."

I laughed. "Me. You ran into a cement box with a woman who knows what you are and how to kill you."

Reoul smiled slyly. "What you don't know will kill you."

I dashed toward the black car as he lunged for me.

CHAPTER 20

The bifron dropped his Dr. Clemons skin suit as he lunged with his claws extended. Despite his pasty skin and thin limbs, he was fast, and he bumped the Mercedes, activating the alarm system. He effectively cut me off from my destination. The noise would effectively draw my doppels back here, but I didn't want them in the way when I got to my car.

I had instructed them in the text to retrieve my vehicle and park it in the garage, but I couldn't be a hundred percent sure he would take this route, so I asked them to watch the main entrance for Dr. Clemons. The bifron had no idea he was walking into a trap, but getting him here and killing him were two different things. He was far more intelligent, and his acting skills were academy-award level after that incident with the cops.

I moved to the opposite side of the car and walked around it, as Reoul did the same. Having the metal between us gave little sense of security, but the bifron appeared to enjoy this game of cat and mouse as he smiled and licked his lips often.

"What is so special about this vehicle? Is this where you are concealing the Ax of Ameron?" Reoul asked.

Carnell hadn't told me the name of the ax, but I slipped it

from my inside jacket and flipped it in my hand. "You mean this old thing? I just wanted you to think you had a fighting chance."

Reoul clasped his hands together. "I have wanted to get my hands on that weapon. The New King will reward me for such a find."

"What is this New King's name again? You were trying to infer it was a she," I said, while holding the ax by its smooth wooden handle.

"Your species is overly concerned about male and female. Such an inefficient way of reproduction."

I almost laughed. He definitely reproduced far easier than the rest of us, but considering the difference in process, I would take the good old fashion way. "Maybe, but it's a lot more fun than throwing up."

The bifron made his way to the hood of the Mercedes, but as he rounded the corner, I popped my trunk. I only had a split second to embed my ax and since Reoul said he wanted it, I arched my arm back and tossed the ax toward him with all my strength. It circled in the air as he held up one hand, but the blade rotated over his thin limb and embedded in the breastbone.

Reoul screamed and staggered backward, gripping the wooden handle with both hands as he tried to dislodge the weapon. I knew I didn't have much time, and I flipped back the black blanket and grabbed the flame thrower.

I slipped the thick strap over my shoulder and hoisted it from the trunk. My finger slipped over the trigger and the barrel grazed the edge of the vehicle as I pulled it free. I clicked the trigger halfway to ignite the pilot inside the barrel. You wouldn't see the small flame, but it was there, ready to do unimaginable damage.

Reoul saw Texas in my arms and darted for the nearest vehicle. I couldn't run fast with the flame thrower but the doppels were staking out the upstairs door to the Moreau building and I was standing in front of the lone vehicle entrance. My demon

DON'T COUNT YOUR DEMONS BEFORE THEY HATCH

friend had to fight one of us and hopefully the doppels locked the stairway to the garage as I asked.

There was a crashing sound as my gaze flew over a row of parked vehicles. Most were black and a cascade of glass crystals tinkled along the cement ground as I inched closer. Reoul wasn't the type to vandalize a car without reason. He was either baiting me or he found something he could use against me.

I couldn't control what people kept in their cars, but I was aware it was more than likely that somebody had a weapon stashed. He didn't need to kill me. He just needed to distract me from the exit so he could escape. I doubted he was enjoying our cat-and-mouse game now. He wasn't used to being the mouse.

Reoul stepped from behind a navy-blue Cadillac. The ax was still embedded in his chest, but despite what I was told, I feared the demon would dislodge it eventually. He had one hand behind his back, and I was pretty sure he had found a knife or tire iron. Giving ground wasn't an option, so I aimed the flamethrower at him and waited for him to come into range.

"You didn't think it would be this easy, did you, Faith?" Reoul asked in a conversational tone.

My finger balanced on the trigger, a hair's breadth from firing as I smiled at him. "Actually, you are quite difficult to kill. The flame thrower would be enough for most demons, but you have some kind of internal husk that needs to be compromised. Fortunately, the ax takes care of that."

Reoul touched the handle of the ax with one hand. "It's true. Demon-blessed weapons stay the healing process, but you do not have these advantages."

"Why would I need one when I am the one holding the flamethrower?"

Everything happened at once. I saw the flash of the gun barrel as he raised the hand he had behind his back. There was no point in trying to avoid the bullet. I only had one chance at my foe. If he dropped me, he was gone.

I lunged forward, so I went to one knee before pressing the trigger of the flamethrower. It exploded in a stream of white and orange flame as the bullet punctured my left shoulder.

The bullet shredded my flesh as it burst from my back and punctured a cement post behind me. But I kept my finger firmly in place as the steam of fire engulfed the bifron.

His arms flailed above him as the screaming echoed in the parking garage, but he fervently fell to his knees, and I released the trigger as the smell of burned flesh made my already rolling stomach heave.

I dropped Texas on the ground with a loud thud as I fell to my back. The shouts were distant at first, but I would recognize my doppels' voices anywhere. My Mercedes alarm was still going off, and I was sure they would be on their way shortly.

Dran was at my side, pulling me to a sitting position before I groaned, and he realized I was bleeding from the ripped leather on my shoulder.

"What happened?" he asked, while inspecting my wound.

"The damn bifron shot me. All this supernatural bounty hunting and I get popped by a measly gun."

Dran held a potion to my lips, and I drank it without another word. The fire in my shoulder began to dissipate instantly and I would have kissed Eve for her potion skills had she been there. "Is that better?"

"Yeah, but you boys need to work on your timing. Since you are here, can you make sure nobody sees that?" I motioned to the barbecued bifron whose black, charred skin was sending off tendrils of steam.

Drin walked to the front of the parking garage and opened a panel. He punched in a code and silver doors slid down, sealing off the entrance.

"It would have been a lot easier if I knew I could do that," I said with mild irritation.

Dran helped me to my feet as Cal and Carnell exited the stairwell that led to the garage. "If I knew you needed the security code for the parking garage, I would have given it to you."

Yeah, that was fair. I had to learn that my adopted family was there for me in any capacity I needed and to trust they had my back. "I will be more forthcoming in the future, but I wasn't sure this was his destination until he arrived. It was a guess."

Carnell glanced at the bloody bullet embedded in the cement post. "You need to trust your instincts, Faith."

"I do," I said.

"Enough to share your plans so we can help you. This aspiring King took a hell of a chance of releasing a bifron. It's a death penalty in the Underworld for such an infraction. Who knows what this demon has planned next?"

"Okay." I took a calming breath as the shredded tissue in my shoulder continued to heal. "I had a conversation with Reoul. That was the bifron's name."

Cal arched an eyebrow. "Only emperors have names. This demon was one of the bifron elders."

"Yeah. He told me that. He had some savvy shifting skills, but he was too adept in our world. When I asked him about it, he told me that he was trained. Someone in the Underworld isn't just releasing these demons into our world. They are training them to adapt and thrive here. That means the aspiring King of Hell is very comfortable in our world and visits often enough to keep up on modern tech and customs."

Carnell rubbed his chin. "You are right. A bifron should not have been that familiar with a gun. He understood how to read a map and how to travel to his destinations without being detected."

"He understood police procedure as well. This isn't like auditing a class in college. The bifron knew exactly what he was doing here."

"We will look into it. I have contacts in the Underworld. Did he tell you anything else that may lead to his employer?" Carnell asked.

"I called our aspiring King a him and Reoul asked why I assumed the new King was male. While I associate the demon rulers as an old boys' club, the bifron doesn't have any gender alliance. He was a master at misdirection, so it may not mean anything, but are any of the Kings female."

Cal shook his head. "No. The Underworld has archaic rules. A demon is required to kill a former King to take his place. There is no female strong enough for such a feat."

"That kind of thinking will have the Underworld females rising up to take power, eventually. But this aspiring King could be anyone. They have proven the lengths they will go to in order to secure power. They may not have much power in the Underworld, but they have gained some here. We have no idea who is helping this King or why, but that dark witch is one of them."

"Dagna will be brought to justice soon. Everyone is looking for her and Greyson is attempting to track her use of dark magic," Carnell said.

The mention of my sexy warlock sent a rush of blood through my veins, but since my shoulder was still in the process of healing, it was accompanied by a dull ache. I rubbed the affected area to attempt to alleviate it.

Cal touched my arm gently. "Do you have any leads on the artifact? This King has four out of the five pieces. The hostages will be kept safe until the ritual, but he or she only needs one more and to perform the rite."

"The demon behind this is smart. The hostages are portaled away the moment the shard is complete. The shrouded thing that took the shard I intercepted was working for this new King. We have to find the acolytes of this aspiring King."

"There is only one location left, Faith. Since this rite was performed in Canton, that leaves only one location before the last ritual, which will be performed here," Carnell said.

I straightened my leather jacket. "I am well aware, and I will be staking out Knoxville like a fly on shit until the last demon shows up."

"We have no idea what the last demon could be. Each one has been more powerful than the last," Carnell mused.

I cocked my head to the side. "The bifron is isolated and feared by every other species in the Underworld. What could be worse than a demon that can start a disease-infested apocalypse?"

Download the next book in the Shrouded Nation series, All That Glitters is Magic HERE! Then turn the page for a preview.

EXCERPT FROM ALL THAT GLITTERS IS MAGIC HERE BOOK #10

*H*unter bent over and pressed his lips to mine before he sank down on the sofa next to me. He must have sensed my mood because the passionate lip lock ended abruptly and he didn't push me for more. There was no doubt what he wanted when he kissed me like that. Before him, I dreaded having sex with Caton. Hunter had shown me how much pleasure I could experience during intercourse. Seriously, Hunter opened a whole new world for me. As cliché as it was, Caton was a selfish lover and never bothered with making sure I enjoyed myself. Normally, I was all for naked gymnastics with my guy. However, the fight in the cave was still too raw for me to get in the mood.

"Has Nishi moved? Or did she put that on hold?" Hunter's fingers played over my shoulder.

My heart clenched when I thought of what my best friend was going through. Nishi's boyfriend was killed recently in a fight against Rerek, the God of Chaos. I was new to having a best friend and not entirely certain how much I should push her to come out of her shell. She was grieving and racked with guilt over not returning Nathan's love.

"Yeah, I helped her and her hunters move her the day before yesterday."

While I was looking forward to having her stay with me, it had been a blessing that Nishi had already packed her house and had everything organized and ready to go. They say that if you put out what you want in the universe, you get it. Nishi was proof that the concept works. Because Nishi was prepared, she could get her stuff out of her place well before the paperwork went through. Thanks to the fact that she was purchasing a house from one of the shifters, she could move right in. And all we had to do was load up her stuff in Roanoke and unload it at the new house in Ravenholde.

Hunter tucked a hair behind my ear. "You're a great friend. Losing someone you care about takes time to get over. It's even worse for those of us in charge. It's our responsibility to keep those we lead from serious harm. It's a failure on our part when someone dies like Nathan did."

I sucked in a gasp and shoved Hunter's muscular chest. "This is not Nishi's fault. She did everything she could. It was Rerek and his damned followers. It could have been any of us."

Hunter cupped my cheeks. "You misunderstood me. Nishi is one of the best leaders I've ever known. Artemis couldn't have selected a better person for the job. It's something we take on ourselves. I was trying to help you understand her guilt."

I nodded, leaving it at that. As someone Nishi trusted, I knew there was more to it than that. And as much as I loved Hunter, I wasn't going to correct his assumption. "Sounds like I need to give her time. Is it bad if I go check on her and try to get her to come for dinner? I can't stand the thought of leaving her to go through this completely alone."

"You should do what you think is best. Your kind heart is what made me fall in love with you in the first place. It's the same for Nishi and Faith, for that matter. It might be helpful to get her focused on banishing Rerek. It's the only revenge she will be able to get."

That reminded me of what we needed to focus on. As much as I wanted to sink into Hunter's side and watch a movie, we couldn't afford to do that. "How do we stop him? He was almost through that portal, and there was nothing I could do to stop him. I cast every spell I could think of to shove him back to his realm and nothing worked."

Hunter pulled his cell phone out and typed something into the screen, then gave me one of his sexy smirks. "I don't have the answers, but I know where to get them." His phone beeped, and he turned the screen to me.

I understood his smirk. Carnell's library was a great resource and was also a dangerous place for us. Hunter and I had given into the effects of the incubus hormones infused in the walls and floor and had sex among the stacks of books. It horrified Faith and amused Carnell.

"If I wasn't so worried about Nishi, I would have thought of using his books," I admitted.

Hunter helped me off my couch and downstairs. We left through the front of my closed store. The moon was full overhead and bathed us in its powerful glow. Hunter paused for a second before he climbed into the truck and backed out of the parking spot. "Should you be running with the pack tonight?" The moon didn't force shifters to change forms, but it did invigorate them.

Hunter shook his head as he sped to the Moreau Building. "Reed is handling the hunt tonight. My wolf would be restless if I were anywhere else but with you."

There had never been a time in my life when I was the priority for anyone. I loved knowing what I needed was important to him. Hunter was a man of action rather than words. "Is that because he claimed me?" I was still learning about shifters. They kept the more intimate details to themselves.

"That and because we both hate being away from you." Hunter pulled behind the tall building.

My heart skipped a beat. We hadn't talked about where we would live after we got mated. Chicken shit that I was, I didn't bring up the subject as he stopped next to the twin doppelgangers that worked for Carnell.

"Hello, beautiful. Always nice to have you visit. How's Nishi? We're thinking of her," Drin or Dran said as he helped me out of the truck.

I chuckled and grabbed Hunter's hand as he led us inside while his brother parked the car. "We got Nishi moved to her new house. She's lying low for now. I'll tell her you want to see her."

"We can get her mind off her grief if she'd give us a chance," the doppel winked at me as the elevator doors closed.

I shook my head and leaned my head on Hunter's shoulder, needing the moment of reprieve. There was no way Nishi would entertain the idea. She was carrying too much guilt for that.

Cal greeted us as the doors opened on the penthouse. "Carnell tells me you're going to be searching for information on Rerek and how to force him back into his realm. You'll need to reinforce the shield, keeping him inside too."

We followed the gargoyle past the leopard print sofa and Carnell's office to the library. The smell of old parchment and leather greeted us. The scent reminded me of our family grimoire. I loved looking through the book and learning the spells of my ancestors. My mother always hovered over me, making sure I didn't damage the book. Eventually, I started one of my own, documenting as many as I could remember from the one my mother refused to let out of her sight.

Cal offered to look with us and the three of us went to the stacks and pulled several volumes that would hopefully give us some information. We worked in silence for over an hour before Cal called and asked for drinks to be delivered. I was sipping a glass of wine when Hunter pointed at the information in one of the books.

"It says here that the gods possessed the ability to shroud themselves in a cloak of invisibility or disguise, allowing them to move amongst humans undetected. They would often take on human forms or appear as ordinary beings to avoid drawing attention to their true divine nature. I bet life was crazy during that time," Hunter mused.

Cal tipped his beer bottle at Hunter. "The gods seldom interacted directly with humans. They preferred to work through intermediaries, such as demigods, heroes, or messengers. They wanted to remain mysterious and divine. They could also influence events from behind the scenes easier this way."

How long had Cal been alive? Was he saying this because he was around then? "Did you ever meet the gods?"

Cal drained his beer, then set the bottle down. "The gods resided in secluded realms or sacred locations, hidden away from the mortal world. Mount Olympus is one example. It's Zeus's home and a meeting place of the Greek gods. Like all others, it's inaccessible to ordinary humans."

That didn't tell me if Cal was around during that time. He was enigmatic. I returned to my reading and noted that when the gods did intervene in human affairs, they often did so through natural events or phenomena. A storm or earthquake was often interpreted as a sign or manifestation of divine will. There were other incidences, like crops dying or thunderstorms, that made people link them to a direct interaction with a specific god.

As I read through a section on mysterious or symbolic manifestations, I found myself praying I would have a prophetic dream, vision, or sign. Preferably one that didn't require interpretation. I scanned through numerous accounts of the gods, adding an element of mystique to their messages and making it difficult for humans to comprehend their true meaning and identities.

It made sense that they operated this way. It made their worshippers even more devout. It also helped the gods maintain their secrecy and keep their celestial presence hidden from the majority of humankind. That allowed them to influence human affairs without disrupting the balance between the mortal and divine realms.

Cal tapped the book in front of him. "This book mentions that after the gods agreed and sealed themselves off, ~~that~~ only objects of power would allow them to interact with our world."

Hunter grabbed a bottle and twisted off the cap. "Why would they do that if the idea was to keep from causing problems on Earth? I'm surprised more gods and goddesses haven't come here and messed with us before now. I hear they get really bored."

I got up and walked around the table, and read over Cal's shoulder. "It's not a key they can use to access our realm. This item is an amplifier for the priest to funnel power to Rerek. That's what is allowing him to interact directly with our world. He couldn't have spread the virus without it. The more power he has, the more likely he can force his way through the ward keeping him isolated."

Cal nodded. "There are markings left behind when a talisman that is connected to a god is created. Before we assume the priest is using one, we should verify it was made."

My mind was whirling a million miles an hour, going through the possibilities. "We should look at the last site to see if there is anything there. There was immense power in that location. It could mean something."

Hunter tilted his head and looked at me across the table. "Tell me what I'm looking for and I will check it out."

I narrowed my eyes at him. "I'm not a porcelain doll that needs to be handled with kid gloves. I can go there without breaking down. Nishi would be another matter, given the circumstances, but I can do my job."

"It's not actually your job, though," Hunter pointed out.

I pursed my lips and crossed my arms over my chest. "I took on the role when I created the cure and the council refused to even acknowledge the problem. I'm a store owner, but also part of this investigative team of middle-aged women that has formed in Ravenholde to solve the Nation's problems. You might question my sanity, but I love being a part of things, and I'm damn good at what I do."

One of Hunter's eyebrows rose, and a smile curved one corner of his lips. "Badass and sexy. How did I get so lucky?" He whistled and gave me a once-over with heat in his eyes. "Okay, what's the plan?"

"The priority should be on finding the talisman that is fueling Rerek. With it, I can cut him off. Once that happens, I can cure the sick and eliminate the spread of the virus. Without that giving him an opening, he won't be able to keep infecting others. It's Rerek's powers that mutated the virus and enabled it to infect supernaturals." I gave Hunter a pointed look. Part of me thought he should have known that, while another said he wasn't familiar with magic and how things like that worked.

Cal shut the book and stood. "I will leave this part to you two. I have shit to do." The gargoyle walked out of the room, leaving me and Hunter staring at one another.

Hunter got up with the sinuous grace of his animal. "You are sexy when you get riled up."

I held up a hand. "No. We aren't giving in again. Let's go check the cave. The priest couldn't exactly gather all of his belongings when he fled. Not to mention that the site was far more elaborate than the others. It could very well be the place they created the talisman."

Hunter wrapped an arm around me and nuzzled my neck as we headed out of the library. "Are you sure you want to go back there?"

I nodded. "I can handle it."

Hunter grimaced as the elevator opened. "Reed told me the council hasn't gotten around to clearing the place out yet."

I rolled my eyes as the doors opened. One of the doppelgangers was there with his smile. "Did you find what you were looking for?"

I lifted a shoulder. "Maybe. We're about to follow up on a lead right now."

The doppel's twin was standing by the passenger door. He extended a hand, then brought mine to his lips for a kiss. "Happy hunting."

Hunter growled as he got into the driver's side and pulled away. I reached for his hand. "You know they mean nothing by their flirting, right? They started it to make me feel better when Caton left me."

Hunter shook his head. "If you believe that, you're sorely mistaken. Those two would have you in their bed if you even hinted at an interest."

His surliness and the truth I heard in his words made me smile. "I can't help it if I'm sexy, Hunter." I was teasing. I'd never felt attractive before he fell for me. The days of feeling like a frumpy middle-aged woman were long gone for me. My self-confidence was growing, but I would never be a self-absorbed bitch like Lucinda.

That made him laugh. "No, you can't. Just don't forget that you're mine, Buttercup."

"Never," I vowed as he pulled over and parked the truck. We would have to hike the rest of the way. My back ached as I hopped out. The discomfort was all in my head because of the last time we'd been out here. Ignoring how the ache moved to my chest, I did a few stretches and was ready to go.

Hunter was like a dog on alert as we headed through the forest to the cave where Nathan had been killed. We encountered a few of his wolf sentries and closer,; we came across some of Caton's lackeys. I suppose that wasn't a fair description. The warlocks had acted as guards for the council for years. They just didn't have stuff to do very often, so they weren't all that disciplined.

"What are you doing back here? Are you the ones that are going to handle the bodies?" One of the warlocks asked us.

Hunter glared at the guy. "No. That's Caton's job. We are here to investigate a lead on the god. All we need to do is look through the site. Has there been any trouble? Did any of the priests come back?"

The warlock shook his head. "We thought we heard something inside an hour ago, but didn't see anything."

"Did you go inside and look around?" I asked. It was important to be clear on what they did and didn't do.

"We went back as far as we could but didn't see anything," the guy replied.

Hunter inclined his head and proceeded into the cave. My stomach lurched when I noted the priests and followers were lying where they'd fallen. The stench had bile playing chicken with the back of my throat. I held my breath and cast a spell to move the decay out through the entrance.

"We're going to have to search each of these priests." I shuddered at the thought of actually touching them.

Hunter nudged my shoulder. "I'll move them outside where we can burn them. Caton isn't going to get to this before we have a bigger mess on our hands."

I smiled up at him. "My hero. But that won't be necessary. I can use a spell to levitate the bodies. We can ask the warlocks to search them."

Hunter chuckled, then he pressed his lips to mine. It took a second for me to ignore the negative energy filling the cavern so I could cast my spell. Levitation was a difficult spell to master. I could do it, but it wasn't easy. It was a gift that some witches possessed and one I'd wished for many times throughout my life. It would have made dusting my store much easier.

Sweat dotted my forehead as I lifted the first body and floated it outside. Hunter went out and told the warlocks to search for any talismans or enchanted objects. While I moved the dead, Hunter searched the floor, walls, and ceiling. He hadn't understood why I asked him to look up. He didn't think they could get up there to carve runes, and he bitched as he used his claws to climb the tallest stalagmites to get a view. That had made me laugh and lose control of my spell. I discovered the limbs were easier to move. They held less of Rerek's evil energy.

Hunter was brave enough to search every crack he could find while I continued the grueling work of moving bodies. I was beginning to lose hope that we would find anything. Every time I lifted a body, I said a little prayer that we would see the symbols to confirm a talisman was made. Having the symbols would help me scry for its location.

Hunter pressed a kiss to my forehead and walked outside to talk with the warlocks as the last body floated. I scanned the area and grimaced at the amount of blood covering everything. Blood magic was dangerous stuff, so I sent my hellfire throughout the space. The whoosh of flames followed a few seconds later. That priest would never be able to use this spot again.

"I'm going to walk through the back tunnels and make sure we didn't miss anything," I told Hunter when he returned.

"I was just about to do that," he said.

I used my magical senses to pick up any significant concentrations of power. There was nothing really until we reached the end, where only a toddler would be able to fit through the crack.

"There is a lot of power here. Was there anything on the other side?"

Hunter shook his head. "Not that I could find. I can break away the top layers of rock and see if anything is hidden beneath that."

"No, don't bother. It's not here. The residual energy isn't high enough." I wiped the sweat from my forehead with the back of my arm.

It had taken us several hours of moving bodies, searching them, and scouring every nook and cranny of the caves. "There's nothing here. Are you sure you don't want me to break the rock away where the tunnel narrows?" Hunter asked. We'd sensed a concentration of power in that spot but found nothing obvious.

"No. I'm certain it was Rerek helping his head priest get away. He needs to keep the guy. He's the only one strong enough to go up against an alpha shifter." My face crumpled, and I fought the urge to whine as I said, "I'm going to have to go back to every location we've ever encountered the priests." That was a lot of shit to have to revisit.

DOWNLOAD the next book in the Shrouded Nation series, All That Glitters is Magic HERE!

ABOUT THE AUTHORS

Reviews are like hugs. Sometimes awkward. Always welcome! It would mean the world to us if you can take five minutes and let others know how much you enjoyed our work. Read on for more information about the two of us and other books we have to offer.

Click here to leave your review!

BRENDA TRIM

Brenda is a USA Today bestselling author that loves everything fantasy and paranormal. She has written over forty books with plans for many more to come. Her series includes the bestselling Dark Warrior Alliance, Midlife Witchery, Mystical Midlife in Maine, Twisted Sisters' Midlife Maelstrom, the Hollow Rock Shifters, and Bramble's Edge Academy.

Brenda creates worlds that feature dangerously handsome heroes and feisty heroines. With the help of popcorn and candy, she takes dragons, fairies, witches, vampires, and so much more and brings them to life. She lives in Texas with her husband and three kids who fuel not only her heart but her life.

If she's not writing, she's reading, traveling, or knee-deep in projects with her husband and five sisters. She encourages readers to Dream Big. If your dreams don't terrify and electrify, you then they aren't big enough!

CLICK THE SITE BELOW TO STALK BRENDA:
Amazon

Bookbub
Facebook
Brenda's Book Warriors FB Group
BooksproutGoodreads
Instagram
Twitter
Website

TIA DIDMON

Tia Didmon is a USA Today bestselling author of provocative paranormal romance. When Tia isn't busy writing about sexy shifters and dreamy demons, she spends her time binge watching The Order and reruns of The Vampire Diaries, cooking with her daughter, and serving her cat. Her love of writing stems from a self-diagnosed book addiction.

Subscribe to Tia's newsletter at tiadidmon.com for a free book and start your journey through Tia's supernatural world today!

CLICK THE SITE BELOW TO STALK TIA:
Amazon
Facebook
Twitter
Website
Instagram
Bookbub
Goodreads
Booksprout
LinkedIn
Tia's tribe Facebook group

ALSO BY BRENDA TRIM

CLICK HERE FOR A COMPLETE LIST OF THE HUNDRED PLUS OTHER TITLES I HAVE AVAILABLE IN PARANORMAL WOMEN'S FICTION & PARANORMAL ROMANCE!

ALSO BY TIA DIDMON

Tia has written over 60 books. CLICK HERE for a complete list and reading order.